THE LONG SEARCH

Center Point
Large Print

Also by Hunter Ingram and available from Center Point Large Print:

Fort Apache
Man Hunt

THE LONG SEARCH

HUNTER INGRAM

Center Point Large Print
Thorndike, Maine

This Center Point Large Print edition
is published in the year 2025 by arrangement with
Golden West Inc.

The text of this Large Print edition is unabridged.
In other aspects, this book may vary
from the original edition.
Printed in the United States of America
on permanent paper sourced using
environmentally responsible foresting methods.
Set in 16-point Times New Roman type.

ISBN: 979-8-89164-488-5

The Library of Congress has cataloged this record
under Library of Congress Control Number: 2024949800

ONE

The smell of the traders' camp wrapped around a man before he reached it. It was made of several odors; the heavy, dry smell of dust that made a man want to choke against it, the rich, pungent smell of oxen manure that twitched at a man's nose, and the lighter smell of unwashed clothes and bodies lacing through it all. The fainter smells that occasionally came to a man were the resin and tallow used in greasing axles.

The unwashed bodies and clothes had the least volume, Wiley Anderson thought, but he found it the more offensive. Maybe it was because he was so conscious of it. The crowded brick barracks of Fort Leavenworth, Kansas, was permeated with the same smell, and he had spent the last two weeks in them. He could say one thing in favor of the camp; the smell wasn't as overpowering as it was in the barracks.

He could hand the traders' camp another credit too. Their camp was comparatively quiet. The traders used oxen to haul their wagons; the army used mules. When night came, oxen lay down and chewed their cud. A mule liked to hear the sound of his own voice, and he could wreck the peace of a night with his braying. Put dozens of them together and they talked back and forth all night long.

He moved down the orderly lines of the white-topped Conestogas. He didn't want to give a trader a damned thing, but he had to say they kept a neater camp than the army did. He didn't want to defend the army, he thought sourly. He had about as much use for it as he had for the traders.

Somewhere around three hundred wagons were in the encampment, and it took a lot of seeking direction to find a single outfit. Some of the eyes, where he stopped, were hostile, and others were indifferent. Some didn't answer him at all, and he suspected others gave him wrong directions, for he found himself retracing steps.

He made an additional effort and held onto his temper, but he didn't know how much longer he could go on. He knew the surly regard the traders had for the army, and they were dumping a lot of it onto him. It wasn't his fault that they couldn't move on to Santa Fe until the army said so, even though he wore a uniform. General Kearny had given those orders; not him.

"Myrick Dorsett's wagons?" He stopped and repeated the question again. He didn't expect to find Dorsett, but he did hope to locate Dorsett's partner here.

The trader started to jeer at him, but something in those smoldering eyes stopped him. This one had been pushed close to the edge.

"Dorsett ain't here," he growled.

"I didn't ask for him," Wiley snapped. "I asked for his wagons." He knew Dorsett wouldn't be foolish enough to come anywhere near here. But he did hope to learn from his partner where Dorsett was.

The trader pulled at his beard, then decided against the anger Wiley's tone put in him. "The damned army thinks it bosses everything. Hendricks got the last wagons in the last row."

Wiley turned away without nodding or saying his thanks. He didn't know this Hendricks at all, and Dorsett only through having seen him. The trader caravan had made up at Independence, and Wiley had searched through it, looking for Dorsett. Neither Hendricks nor Dorsett had been with it. It seemed that Wiley's information that Hendricks had joined the caravan at Leavenworth was right.

At this moment his face was harsh and impassioned. He was above average height and hewn lean. He moved with a long stride, giving the impression of more vigor than grace. He was like a half-grown bear cub, with the suggestion of power still hidden by awkwardness. His cheeks were hollowed under the sharp, prominent cheekbones, and his black hair was long, reaching down to his collar and hiding his ears. He guessed he should have gotten it cut before joining up, but a bottom farmer stretched his pennies as far as he could.

His dark eyes shadowed with the worry about what would happen to that farm while he was gone, and it was an additional burden to all the other worries he carried. A man beat himself to pieces toting the bag of troubles heaped on him.

How many times had he asked himself what he was doing in this ill-fitting uniform, and the answer was always the same. With the war between the United States and Mexico, the normal route to Santa Fe was cut off. If a man wanted to reach it, he traveled with the army, and putting on the uniform was the only way he knew to assure that.

Last winter's spell of ague fever had left its stamp on him, and his face was just getting back its normal color. That had been a bad attack, and he had dragged around for weeks. The doctors hadn't been able to do much about the fever; a man made it or he didn't. He looked back to the time with no relish. He had frozen one moment and burned up the next.

He shook his head. He never heard of anybody who knew what caused it. One guess was as good as another. Some said it came out of the soil, others that the river's damp mists carried it. It left a man weak as a kitten, and it turned his face yellow. He hoped he would never have another bout with it, but he doubted that he would be that lucky. He had seen too many members of his family carried off by it, and each loss had added to the sweeping tide of loneliness. Then he had met Linda, and the loneliness was gone.

His soul writhed in sudden anguish. He didn't have too much of that period of happiness to remember. He had held her a little over a year, and he would never forget the shock of her leaving him. A man could live with a woman and not have the slightest knowledge of what was in her head. Oh, he had known she was unhappy and complained constantly, and it had only driven him to harder effort. But nothing he did seemed to satisfy her. At first the grief of her leaving him was uppermost, then the hate had slowly risen to drown the first emotion. She and Dorsett had thoroughly stripped him, leaving him only the farm, with not enough money to run it. The hating had become uppermost in his life; he only wanted to catch up with them, not to regain his money for he had no doubt that was gone. The revenge would be only partial payment for the loss he had suffered. He had spent a futile trip to St. Louis because of a worthless lead, then he had picked up this second one.

The report said she was in Santa Fe with Myrick Dorsett. Wiley was going to Santa Fe to kill Dorsett. Could he kill Linda? During some of the black, lonely hours the answer was yes. The daylight always weakened it. Maybe killing Dorsett was all the vengeance he could wreak upon her. Maybe he could do no more to her than leave her grief-stricken and dependent in a foreign city. He wasn't yet ready to face a definite answer. It depended upon how deeply the poisoned roots of his hating dug into his mind.

Killing Dorsett would be pure pleasure. Dorsett had put those wild-flighted thoughts into her head. She had listened to Dorsett's talk of travel, of the wonderful things to be seen. Dorsett was a trader, and Wiley's hatred of him rubbed off onto all traders. Dorsett had the gift of gab, and men and women flocked around him, listening spellbound to him. Wiley should have seen what was forming, but he was too blind. One morning he had gotten up, and she was gone. He would never know how she had slipped out of the house without his hearing her.

He was twenty-four years old, though the somber cast of his face made him look ten years older. He would have been in Santa Fe before now, if it weren't for this war. He wasn't mad at those Mexicans. Come to think of it, he didn't even remember ever seeing one. He knew they lived many miles to the southwest and as long as they stayed down there he didn't care what they did. He had intended taking off for Santa Fe alone, and the war had broken out. He knew how dangerous that would be. Besides, he didn't have the money to make the trip, and volunteering for the army solved a problem. It also covered another angle; joining the army offered him protection. He would stay with it until he caught up with Dorsett and Linda.

The traders were parked outside of Leavenworth, fretting for the time for the army to march. Kearny said they couldn't leave until he gave the orders, and the general had the final say. The traders wouldn't go into Santa Fe again until the army entered it. Kearny's popularity with the traders was as feeble as it was with the volunteers.

That was the traders' problem. Wiley guessed what he intended doing would be called desertion. He didn't give a damn what the army thought.

He found the five wagons in the last row, and the gray-haired man was bending over a kettle suspended over a fire beside the lead wagon. The aroma of cooking meat drifted from it. Five bullwhackers squatted on their haunches, their faces hungry. Tough men, Wiley decided. They looked it, with faces bearded and their clothes well-worn and dirty.

The gray-haired man looked up at the sound of Wiley's steps, and the beginning of a friendliness faded from his face as he saw the uniform.

"I thought this was off limits for you soldiers."

Wiley's face darkened. He was a Missouri volunteer, and there was a vast difference between being a volunteer and a regular. Kearny had issued orders against the Army of the West going into the traders' camp, but then he had regulations for doing everything, including a man wiping his backsides.

"Are you Hendricks?" If Wiley had ever heard Hendricks' first name, he didn't remember it.

Hendricks straightened, and his lips curled. "What's it to you?"

He must have been prematurely gray, for his face didn't show that much aging. Wiley would put him somewhere around forty, but that wasn't enough to slow him too much. He was a chunky man, well-muscled and with a positive manner. Trading was a hard life, making exacting demands upon a man, and this one looked as though he could handle whatever came along. This was Dorsett's partner, and it wasn't hard for Wiley to transfer his feeling from Dorsett to him.

His staring must have prickled Hendricks' nerves, for he demanded, "Who in the hell are you?"

The bullwhackers watched with delight the exchange of hostility between them. If it went beyond that, Wiley had picked himself some sorry odds.

"Anderson. Wiley Anderson."

Hendricks tried to keep his face blank, but he couldn't keep the flicker of emotion from his eyes. The name meant something to him.

"Never heard of you."

No matter how much he tried to deny it, he was a liar.

"You heard of me." Hendricks had doubtless heard about Linda too, but Wiley couldn't mention her name before all of them. "Where's Dorsett?"

Hendricks shrugged, and the gesture was too elaborate. "We split up a long time ago. Haven't heard of him in months."

Wiley decided there was a smirk in Hendricks' voice. Hendricks knew all about this affair, where Dorsett was and that Linda was with him.

"You know where he is. Santa Fe, isn't it?"

Hendricks' jaw hardened. "Are you calling me a liar?"

"A goddamned liar."

"Why, damn you," Hendricks roared and plunged around the fire.

Wiley planted himself. The man built up a quick head of steam, he thought. And it seemed he grabbed at any excuse to cut it loose. The bullwhackers straightened, their eyes glistening. If they took a hand in this, Wiley stood in a poor way.

He threw a looping right hand, catching Hendricks flush in the middle of the beard. It was a good blow; he felt the shock of it run along his arm. He might look deceptively thin, but those long sloping shoulders carried power.

Hendricks' feet flew from under him, and he

landed on his back. His head slammed against the ground, puffing up dust from beneath it. His mouth was open, but no sound came from it. He tried to lift his head, and his eyes were glassy.

Wiley waited for him to get to his feet. Maybe it would have been smarter if he stomped him, but he had to keep an eye on those bullwhackers. They had made no move as yet. He hoped they would stay out of it; at least until he had handled Hendricks.

"Shall I take him for you, boss?" one of them asked.

Hendricks' eyes turned small and mean as his senses returned. He cursed with breath he needed; he cursed the bullwhacker, and he cursed Wiley.

Wiley's face remained impassive under the flood of invective. Hendricks knew all the words.

Hendricks' effort to rise broke on the first attempt. He made it the second time, though his legs were shaky. His breathing rasped as he gulped for air.

He shook his head, and a few drops of blood flew. "I'm going to break you in two."

He might, Wiley admitted. It wouldn't be the first time it had happened to him. He hadn't intended this to turn this way, and he was sorry about it. Not because he had hurt Hendricks; he wasn't going to get any information out of him, but he could easily get bruises instead.

He let Hendricks come to him and let a pawing

fist slip over his shoulder. Momentum carried Hendricks into him, and Wiley dug for the belly. He already knew that Hendricks' jaw was hard.

He drove his fist deep, and Hendricks' breath exploded in his face. It reeked of stale whisky.

Hendricks was knocked back a couple of wobbly steps. He leaned over, wrapping his arms around his belly. He lost his balance and sat down hard. That blow hurt him more than the first, for his face picked up a greenish cast.

Hendricks didn't like them in the guts; it was something to remember. Wiley watched him and the bullwhackers at the same time. The bullwhackers stirred and muttered angrily. They didn't like the way this was going, either. He heard shouts coming from behind him, and somebody yelled, "Fight." He heard the pound of feet heading in this direction.

"Get up Hendricks," he said. "Get up."

The yelling all around him was louder. This was the focal point of interest for the whole camp. Sure, he felt concern. He was going to have everybody on his shoulders. He had better finish Hendricks off and get him off his hands as fast as he could.

Hendricks showed the effort it took to get to his feet. Each step came down flat-footed, and he carried his hands too low. The greenish tinge was still in his face, and he looked as though he wanted to gag against it.

Wiley threw the cautious waiting aside. He went in straight and hard, and he took a feeble blow on his cheekbone that still carried a sting. He hit Hendricks in the belly again, then lifted his blows to the face. Hendricks was bending forward, and his face was an unprotected target.

Wiley pivoted and got the maximum leverage behind his fist. It straightened Hendricks and sent him back the other way. His eyes rolled up into his head, and he was out before he went down.

Wiley rubbed the ache in his knuckles and waited. The bullwhackers weren't going to let him walk away from here; it was in their faces.

He threw a quick glance about him. Faces were packed in a couple of loose ranks, and they all carried the same hungry gleam. His putting Hendricks on the ground wasn't the answer to the need they felt.

The bullwhackers moved as though by a simultaneous signal. They fanned out as they came toward him, and all of the various angles they took made it that much tougher. Wiley wished he had his rifle with him; the stock of it would be a satisfying thing to swing and make a couple of gaps in that half-circle.

They came in a concerted rush, and he tried to put all his attention on a single face, knowing he would only waste his efforts if he tried to cover all of them at once.

He got in a smashing blow that dropped one of

them to his hands and knees, and the remaining four broke all over him. It was hopeless fighting these odds out in the open; he would have been better off if he could have gotten a wagon at his back.

He took a blow on his ear that raddled his senses and watered his eyes. The fists rained in on him. He thought he must be imagining things; the yelling seemed to have a new, authoritative increase.

The crushing weight was all over him, and their eagerness to get at him got in each other's way and saved him for a few seconds. He fought with his fists, his feet, his knees. He doubled one of them over with a vicious thrust to the groin and knocked another away. For a moment, he thought he might stay on his feet, then they hauled him to the ground. They tried to hit him all at once and blows were muffled by others. But they were getting to him. He couldn't get an unlabored breath of air, and his vision was beginning to black out.

Then it seemed to lessen, and he couldn't understand what was happening. But that weight was being yanked off of him.

"Stop it," a voice roared. "Goddam it, I say stop it."

Wiley had the confused impression of activity all around him. Men were being shoved back, and the yelling and swearing was louder.

He shook his head, trying to clear his eyes, and looked up into the red, angry face of Sergeant Buckley. He had seen Buckley angry many times, but never as angry as this.

"Keep them back," Buckley roared. "Use those rifle butts."

Wiley picked out a half-dozen volunteers behind Buckley, and they were effectively using those rifle butts. The savage jabs of those butts drove the traders back several steps.

Wiley had never been so glad before to see blue uniforms. He guessed the uproar of the fight had reached Buckley and his men on the post.

Buckley reached down and jerked Wiley to his feet. It was hard for Wiley to stand, and he ached all over. A man could take a hell of a beating in a few seconds.

"What the hell do you think you were doing?" Buckley demanded. He was a short man with a permanently burned face and hot blue eyes. He had served four years as a regular, and though he had volunteered to get back in, his contempt for ordinary volunteers had carried over. It shone in his eyes now.

He looked about him, and an unconscious grudging was in his voice. "Though I'll say you did pretty good. Who started it?"

Two dozen voices answered at once. "He did."

Buckley's eyes bored into Wiley.

Wiley jerked his head toward Hendricks. Hendricks was just beginning to stir. “He came after me. I had to stop him.”

Voices all around yelled that he was a liar. Buckley debated it for a moment. “You tell it to Colonel Doniphan. Let him straighten it out.”

It was the best news Wiley had heard in a long time. Doniphan could take a man’s hide off him with eyes and words, but Wiley would still face him to get out of this camp.

TWO

Doniphan's office was in the first barrack in the row. The air in it was hot and stagnant, and the candles gave a poor light. Doniphan had his coat off, and suspenders held up his pants. His eyes looked tired, and his face had a sag. At Buckley's entrance, he laid down a paper he held. He took in Wiley with a single glance.

"What is it, Sergeant?"

Buckley pushed Wiley forward. "Starting a fight in the traders' camp."

"Ah." Doniphan's single word said nothing. "What caused it?"

"I couldn't find out, sir."

"Was he alone?"

"All by himself." A fleeting grin touched Buckley's mouth. "He was giving a pretty good account when we pulled him out of it. But that couldn't have lasted long. They had him down."

Wiley's lip bled, and he could feel the trickle down his chin. It caused him more itching than pain.

"Wipe your chin off," Doniphan ordered.

"Yes, sir." Wiley pulled a handkerchief from his pocket and held it against his lip. Stopping the trickling relieved that prickling itching.

Buckley's face was carefully blank, but it didn't conceal that he was enjoying this. "I thought you would want to handle him, Colonel." His implication said, he's one of your volunteers. He belongs to you.

Doniphan nodded. "I'll take care of it, Buckley."

"Yes, sir." Buckley gave him a smart salute and wheeled. He marched out of the office, and everything about him was what the military man should be.

Wiley caught it, and thought sourly that Buckley was plainly pouring on the difference between them for Doniphan's benefit. Buckley had all the advantage. He hadn't just been in a fight.

Doniphan picked up the paper. "Sit down, Wiley."

Wiley tried not to squirm on the hard chair as the hot office air wrapped around him. Two weeks was about all he could stand of the army's drill-packed days, the noncoms yelling out their lungs, the officers screaming at the noncoms, and Kearny looking madder than anybody else. Kearny's regulars despised the volunteers, and the volunteers didn't think much of the regulars. The cross-purpose was a deep river flowing between them. On the best days, the army couldn't accomplish anything but confusion; the worst ones were chaotic. Most of the drills didn't make sense and before a man could get one through his head, another was hammered at him. The horse drills were worse than the infantry drills; a man on foot could get himself out of one quicker when it went sour. When he was mounted and had a horse to untangle, it really became a madhouse. The officers' and noncoms' faces purpled when a mounted company tried to go in all directions.

Wiley scowled at the floor. What was happening wasn't the volunteers' fault. They were farm boys and small-town clerks, and the army wasn't taking enough time to train them. If the Mexican army was trained and better conditioned, Wiley thought Kearny's Army of the West was going to get its ass kicked off. That wasn't his worry; he hadn't joined to fight the Mexicans. He had joined up only because he could see no better way to get to Santa Fe.

My God, when was Doniphan going to lay down that paper again? This office was as hot as the crowded barracks. The air wasn't as rank with the smell of unwashed bodies, and it was quiet. The babble in the barracks drove Wiley almost crazy. It swirled around him until he wanted to yell at it. It made the Mexicans eight feet tall, carrying knives half that long. With one stroke they could split a man from his crotch to his Adam's apple. Wiley didn't like to hear about it; the thought of it turned his skin clammy. He hated a damned knife. The other subject of talk was worse. When it wasn't the Mexicans, all the men talked about was women. He had the same thing on his mind, but it was in the singular, and he never spoke of it.

Doniphan laid down his paper and held his eyes closed in deep weariness for a moment. "Want to talk about it, Wiley?"

"Nothing to talk about, Colonel."

"Not colonel when we're together, Wiley." A note of exasperation was in Doniphan's voice. "Aleck. You know how I feel about that."

A faint smile touched Wiley's mouth and faded. He knew that. Alexander Doniphan had no affectation in him. It galled the regular officers to see him and his men on this familiar basis.

Doniphan was a huge man, standing six-foot-four inches, taller than any man on the post. His shoulders could jam a wide doorway. He had thin reddish hair and big hands. He seemed almost absent as he let a man talk, but he was judging every word. He had the knack of picking out the weakness in a man's words, and after he was through, he cut him down. He had the background for it. He had built a reputation as a case-winning lawyer, and when he was in a courtroom, he dominated it. Outside of Doniphan's handling the farm deed for him, Wiley had had no other experience with him. He considered him a fair man. Besides, he was a Clay County man, the same as Wiley. He liked and respected him.

Wiley thought he would pry at his refusal to explain, but Doniphan veered so rapidly that it confused him.

"Why did you join, Wiley?"

Wiley lifted his hands. "The same reason as all the other boys."

Doniphan shook his head. "I doubt if any two men in the First Missouri Mounted have the same reason, Wiley."

He paused, and Wiley wondered at the thoughts in his head. He wished Doniphan would end this; he wanted to have his punishment over. How many hours of carrying an earth-filled pack before the guardhouse would he get?

"I heard about the Mexican atrocities, Aleck. I guess it fired my blood. All that mutilating Americans—" he let the rest of it fade.

Doniphan's doubting expression put an aggrieved look on Wiley's face. "I guess they were true, weren't they?"

Doniphan shook his head. "Part of them maybe. In a war, both sides commit them. War strips the veneer of civilization from a man and lets the real animal out."

Doniphan used fancy language. Wiley thought about it before he nodded reluctantly. He wasn't going to try to argue with Doniphan; particularly when it wasn't his reason.

"Do you think that's the only reason the other boys joined up? You're wrong," Doniphan went on before Wiley could answer. "I know some of them. You know Obadiah Shannon?"

Wiley nodded. He knew him but not to his pleasure. Shannon was a tavern bully with heavy fists who liked to inflict pain on a man. Wiley had had one run-in with him, and Shannon had beaten him half-senseless. Wiley stayed out of his path all he could.

"He beat up John Colvin in Liberty. He faced charges until the sheriff told him it might be a good idea if he got out of Clay County for a while. Joining up seemed a convenient solution. Do you think Shannon worried about Mexican atrocities?"

Wiley frowned. He would agree that Shannon had a different reason. He couldn't see what this was leading to.

"Wouldn't you say Ben Marshall is a ladies' man?"

Sure, everybody who knew Marshall's reputation would say that.

Doniphan smiled. "Ben hid under the army's skirts to keep that widow off his back. And young Bodine just wanted to get away from his father's dominance." Doniphan stared unseeingly at his desk top. "Go down the roster, Wiley, and for every name on it you'll find a different reason. What's yours? Or do you even know?"

Wiley was tired of being pushed onto the defensive. "What's yours?" he challenged.

Again, that weary smile showed. "I've wondered about it. My country's at war. Maybe I can't go beyond that."

Anger emboldened Wiley. "Or maybe you got a taste for it against the Mormons." Doniphan had led the Missouri militia against the Mormon town of Far West in Caldwell County. That had been eight years ago, and it had been a bloodless war, for the Mormons had surrendered without firing a shot. The superior Missouri militia force had everything to do with it. Doniphan had withdrawn when higher authority had ordered him to execute the Mormon leaders. Wiley didn't know all the straight about that affair. He knew only that Governor Boggs had wanted the Mormons out of Missouri.

"I was eight years younger," Doniphan said. "A man has a before-and-after view. I wasn't crazy about the responsibilities then, Wiley. And I didn't want them again. I thought I should be in this war but not try to lead it. I enlisted as a private, but you volunteers elected me colonel."

That was true. Wiley could understand the volunteers' view. Who had better experience than Doniphan?

Wiley still felt aggressive. "Are you against this war?" Doniphan sounded as though he was against it. If so, what was he doing in it?

"A hundred men will give you a hundred viewpoints as to how they see this war. Polk annexed

Texas and claimed that the boundary between Mexico and the United States was the Rio Grande River and not the Nueces. I guess Polk saw the chance to grab land. History would mark him down as the President under whom the United States grew. Polk sent Taylor and an army into the disputed strip, and the Mexicans attacked." He spread his hands. "We were in a war as quick as that. Did Polk actually want war? You can get a thousand different views on that too." His face was heavy under some reflection. "But it is an odd thing. Polk is a Democrat. The Democrats make wars, us Whigs fight them."

He smiled as Wiley's face showed that he was trying to puzzle through this. "Check the Missouri volunteers, Wiley. Most of them are Whigs. I am. You're one."

Wiley's frown deepened. He had never even thought about it like this before. He did know about Clay County's company. The preponderance of it was heavily Whig.

"The politicians say it's our manifest destiny, Wiley. It gives them a noble-sounding banner to hide any act we do. We can take another country, we can spoil it. We can break our promises and cheat in our business affairs. And to salve our consciences we say we're taking a better way of life into benighted lands. Sometimes I wonder—" he left it unfinished.

Wiley could imagine Doniphan spent many an

hour trying to figure this out. Doniphan was a thinker; Wiley wasn't. He just wanted to get out of this office.

"Wiley, why did you go into that traders' camp?"

Wiley squirmed. He might have known that Doniphan hadn't forgotten about it. "I just sorta wandered over there."

"Was it Hendricks you fought?"

Wiley tried to hide his surprise. How did Doniphan know that? Buckley hadn't mentioned any names.

"He jumped me."

"After you asked him questions about his partner. Don't look so surprised, Wiley. I knew both of them. Dorsett and Hendricks have been together for several years."

Wiley's face was sullen. "It just happened."

There was almost pity in Doniphan's head-shake. "I knew Linda too. She was a pretty thing. Liberty's a small town. It's hard for a man to keep his personal business hidden."

Wiley didn't speak, and Doniphan sighed. "I'll tell you what I think, Wiley. You're going to Santa Fe for one reason: to kill a man and maybe a woman. I don't know how deep your hating has grown." His eyes bored into Wiley. "Your hating's shown. If you kill either of them, don't you see what will happen? It becomes an army affair. You'll be court-martialed for murder. You know what that means."

Wiley felt the cords in his throat tighten. "God-dam it." He couldn't keep his voice down.

"To bring her back you'd have to desert, Wiley. Is that in your head? You could be shot for that."

Words were damming up behind Wiley's locked lips. He would explode in another few minutes.

"If you're wondering what I'm talking about, Wiley, I worry about every man I have. I hope to get every one of them back."

Doniphan was hemming him in, and Wiley was being driven wild. He couldn't take much more of this.

"Wiley, I'm sorry for you." Doniphan's voice was very quiet. "You're in love with her. And nothing else matters."

The heat in Wiley's face was burning him up. "Is that all, Colonel?"

Doniphan's face looked beaten as he picked up his paper again. "That's all, Wiley."

Wiley took a step, then stopped. "What about tonight?"

Doniphan didn't look at him. "I'm forgetting that it happened."

THREE

Wiley learned that if a man didn't like the rumor he heard, all he had to do was to get another one from the next man. The volunteers speculated on everything that happened and everything that might happen, until a man didn't know which way to turn. He overheard some of the officers' conversations, and they weren't any more positive than the men. He could count on a few facts, the things he had actually seen. The drilling was over, and the Army of the West was on the march. Its destination was Santa Fe, and conjectures were rife that the fighting for New Mexico would be prolonged and hard. General Taylor's Army of Occupation was to strike directly into the heart of Mexico, and General Wood's Army of the Center was to operate against the City of Chihuahua. Wiley didn't know anything about strategy, but he guessed this one was all right. Mexico would be crushed under a three-pronged attack. God knew that the United States should have enough men to do it. Wiley had heard that fifty thousand volunteers had been called in to fill out the regulars. If it was true, it ought be enough to stomp into the sand every Mexican they saw.

He shifted in the saddle to ease his aching

buttocks. The days of the drills, the yelled orders of about-faces and column of fours were over, and he had thought those days were hard. They were play compared to this. One day was like another, each growing worse by the weight of their accumulation. They had plodded across the barren plains of Kansas, spending a good portion of each day hunting for wood and water. Grass was another frightening problem, for it was scarce and wilting under a blazing sun. Those treeless wastes were a region known only to the hunters and trappers. Roads were almost nonexistent and the few that did exist were unmarked. The army couldn't get lost, for the traders had been along that way many times, and the traders' wagons trailed the army's march. Wiley wasted quite a few bitter thoughts on the traders; not because of his personal involvement with a couple of them; but because the traders were here. Business as usual was their only thought. If the army was beaten, they could lose all of their trade goods. If a man counted his life and his freedom important, the loss could be far worse.

Three hundred traders' wagons lumbered along behind the army's supply wagons. Combined, they made a tremendous cloud of dust. Thank God, Kearny had enough sense to let the mounted men ride ahead of the wagons. Nobody had pointed out to Kearny how much more miserable it would be to trail and eat that dust. Wiley almost grinned, remembering last night's argument around the campfires. Some of the volunteers said that Kearny wouldn't do such a thing, and others as vigorously claimed that Kearny just hadn't thought of it.

Daniel Elam rode beside Wiley. His blue shirt was stiffened and whitened under the armpits from his sweating. He didn't ride in somnolent misery as the others did. He had a thin, scrawny neck, and his head constantly turned on it as though there were great sights to be seen. His eyes peered nearsightedly through steel-rimmed glasses, and Wiley would have picked him as the last man to be a soldier. But the army had taken him. He looked ridiculous with that saber hanging from his thin waist, and he was the type of soldier that sergeants enjoyed for he drove them wild. Elam tried harder than any man in the company, but he never got things quite right.

Elam mopped his face. "Hot, isn't it?" That wasn't a complaint; he rarely made one.

It was worse than hot, Wiley thought. Another sandstorm was blowing up. He hoped the wind wouldn't get up to gale proportions. If the velocity was great enough, those stinging particles could peel the hide off a man. His mouth was sore from riding in heat in past storms, and his lips were swollen and parched. His tongue felt slimy, and talking was hard. That was from drinking the bad water, and he thought longingly of the streams and rivers back in Missouri. He remembered the cold sweet spring on his place that only the most severe of droughts could shut off. This damned country had nothing but alkaline and saline water in it.

He moved his lips in a parody of a grin. Elam knew it was hot. Let that answer for him.

"I can't get over seeing Pike's Peak even though it was four days ago," Elam said. He twisted in his saddle for another look.

They had seen it the twenty-eighth of July, and somebody said Pike's Peak was a good hundred miles away. The mountain's peak had loomed up on the horizon so deep purple it looked black. Sure, Wiley had reacted to it; he had never seen it before, but he hadn't gone crazy over it like Elam.

He worked spit around in his mouth to lubricate his tongue. "You should've asked Doniphan to take a side trip so you could see it closer."

Elam grinned at him. "Laugh at me all you want to. But I've never seen anything before. I was born in Liberty, and before I came out here I was never more than a hundred miles away from it. It meant something to me to see that mountain."

He was like a kid in his enthusiasm, and maybe that was the reason he was a good teacher. He would bring back to his class every new or strange thing that he had seen, and his recounting of it would give it shape and form before his class's eyes.

"Is that why you joined up, Dan?"

Elam gave it a moment's sober thought. "How else would I get to see things?"

Doniphan's words came back to Wiley. This was another reason Doniphan had spoken of, and Wiley couldn't say it was less than the other reasons.

He worked his mouth around before he spoke again. "Dan, have you read about New Mexico?"

"Some," Elam admitted cautiously. "Why?"

"I want to know something about it." Wiley knew Elam read a lot, and he trusted him. It was odd asking a man who hadn't seen anything, but then he had education in its place.

"What do you want to know about it?"

Wiley lifted his hands helplessly. "Anything you know. I hear we're getting fairly close to it. Mexicans live there, don't they?"

Elam nodded and eyed him curiously. "Does the thought of it scare you, Wiley?"

"No," Wiley said in sudden anger, then relaxed. He didn't have to put on a big show to impress Elam. "Maybe it does when I get to thinking about it." He didn't plan on fighting them, but if the Mexicans stood between him and Santa Fe, he had to get through them, didn't he? "I've heard those Mexicans are pure hell in a fight. I've never even seen one."

"Me neither, Wiley. But I've never read of them winning too many big, important battles. And they're not eight feet tall as some of the boys say. They're small people by our standards. Their skins are brown, some of them almost black."

"But they carry and use knives." Wiley could express his honest anxiety; he could trust Elam not to rag him.

Elam slapped at a horsefly on his horse's withers and grunted with satisfaction at the smear on his palm. "I've read about them carrying machetes; long, wide-bladed knives they use to clear their land. But it doesn't make sense to me to think they could be of much use against guns."

Wiley's small sigh was relieved. Elam was a comforting man; he picked out the weaknesses in a bigmouth's talk and exposed them. He guessed he would cultivate Elam more. Elam would make better company than some of the others.

Elam was struggling with something, and he blurted it out. "I don't know what I'll do when I have to face them, Wiley. I never killed a man."

Wiley had never killed a man either; in fact he hadn't even thought of it until Dorsett came along. But he had lived with that black thought for a long time now, and it wouldn't be hard to carry it through. Killing depended upon how a man made up his mind. He had already done that about Dorsett. He almost blurted it out, then held it. How would Elam react if he knew the thoughts in Wiley's head? Horror-stricken, he imagined. Violence had never entered Elam's life. Mine neither, Wiley thought angrily. Not until Dorsett crossed my path. No, he couldn't talk about it to Elam. He would be more approachable than Doniphan, but his advice would be the same.

He straightened in the stirrups to ease his aching butt. Wouldn't this day's march ever end? For the last hour he had been hoping Kearny would let up on them. A wind gust caught his saber and whipped it against the back of his legs. He cursed it in sudden rage. That was the most useless damned piece of equipment that was ever handed out to a man. If it wasn't gouging a man, it banged and bumped his legs. Some of the men had thrown them away, then claimed they lost them. Wiley had dutifully hung onto his. He had gone through all the drills showing him how to use it, but he would never be adept with one. He learned how to tie one end of his neckerchief to the saber hilt and the other to his wrist to keep from dropping it. Wiley clung to one positive thought about it; a saber would reach farther than a machete.

The volunteers carried a motley assortment of weapons. Wiley had a Jenks breechloader tucked under his cinch, and Elam had a Hall breech-loader. The army hadn't had enough modern rifles to issue every man one, but most of the volunteers were just as well satisfied. They were used to the Jenks, the Halls, the Eli Whitney factory's rifles and even the ancient flintlocks.

Wiley had heard many an argument over the relative accuracy of an individual's rifle, and each man was ready to demonstrate and prove his weapon the best.

He half-closed his eyes in a stupor of misery and discomfort. Kearny commanded the entire column, but the actual regulars were only the battalion of light artillery from St. Louis, the battalion of Infantry, and the First Dragoons. They'd be in a hell of a shape, Wiley thought sourly, if we weren't along. The artillery trundled twelve six-pounders and four twelve-pounders. He hadn't yet seen the artillerymen fire them, and he wondered if they were any good.

The column was beginning to jam up against some stoppage ahead, and Wiley took hope from it. He looked toward Elam. "Maybe Kearny thinks he's milked everything out of us he can today."

Elam squinted at the setting sun. "I'd say it's about time."

Wiley thought of the evening details to be done before a man could settle down to a little rest. It was worse than a farm's chores. The horses had to be rubbed down, fed and watered, then put on a picket line. An infantryman had it over a cavalryman at the day's end, though Wiley hated walking so much he wouldn't trade places with him.

He leaned over and patted the claybank's neck. "Maybe we can get you a decent drink tonight."

He doubted it, but he could hope. Until he saw the camping spot the scouts picked out.

He swore as he saw the brackish water. He thought it came from an underground seepage, and it spread over a fair area but looked shallow. He wondered if it would last to water all of the animals.

He waded out several steps, wanting to find deeper and better water. He was surprised when it reached almost to his knees.

He spread aside the greenish scum, scowling as he saw the dead insects that floated on the surface. He filled his canteen, and every man did the same before letting the animals drink. Wiley took a meager mouthful and was tempted to spit it out. He swallowed it, and it was no worse than some of the other water they had found.

His boots squished as he waded back out, and the yellow cavalry trimming on his pants was fouled and muddy. He thought the claybank wasn't going to drink, but it did after it tossed its head several times.

He didn't let the horse drink all it wanted. Some of the cavalrymen didn't give a damn, letting an animal take on enough water to bloat it. Wiley cared for his horse more than that. He gave it the best attention he could; even that did little to ease a horse's living in this country.

He looked at Elam's animal. "He's had enough, Dan."

"But he isn't through."

"Do you want to bloat him?" Wiley snapped. He couldn't blame Elam for not knowing any better. Elam wasn't a farm boy. But a lot of the others were, and Wiley saw too much bloating, too many gall sores, and dozens of lame animals.

He prolonged the rubbing down as long as he could before he put the claybank on the picket line. The need for hay tonight would put a heavy drain on the supply wagons. He hoped he would be late enough to miss one of the wood details, but this wasn't one of his lucky nights.

He silently cursed as Buckley picked him on one of the last details going out. Hunting wood was almost a futile thing out here. He thought with regret of all that timber back in Missouri. Finding wood in Missouri was no chore. A man wouldn't have to bend over many times to fill his arms.

He spent a half hour searching, and this wasn't wood; these were puny sticks. He swore at the tiny load he had. Buckley would swear at him for malingering, but he had done the best he could. He wasn't proud of what he had gathered, but no other man of his detail had done any better.

He heard the swearing before he reached the camp, and it didn't seem possible that such a volume came out of a single man.

Buckley was doing the swearing, and he grabbed the detail as it came into view. He yelled, “Drop that wood and put your back into that caisson.”

Wiley swelled with rage as he saw what had happened. Those goddamned artillerymen couldn’t keep their guns out of anything that looked soft. All the way from Leavenworth this had happened at every river crossing, at each piece of soft or boggy ground. Soft ground seemed to be a lure for the artillerymen, and they couldn’t miss one patch of it. They had wheeled one of the guns too near the water, and the long brass twelve-pounder was buried hub-deep and tilted.

Sergeants and officers were gathered around the scene, and they yelled conflicting orders. They had tried to put additional horses on the caisson to yank it out, and that wasn’t any good. The bottom was too soggy for the horses to get enough purchase, and their flailing hoofs churned up a muddy froth and threw it all over everybody within reach.

Somebody finally had enough sense to take the horses out of there before they wore themselves out.

“Move,” Buckley roared at the men he had assembled. “Get that caisson out of there.”

The rage was a poison bubbling in Wiley. That was the army’s way. Put a man to doing what a horse couldn’t. Sheer muscle power was expected to lift the caisson out of this muck and onto firmer ground. He was on a wheel opposite Elam, and it was too bad Elam had gotten caught for this. His scrawny frame wasn't equal to what was being asked from him.

Obadiah Shannon was right behind Elam, and he was the kind of man Buckley should have picked for this. Shannon wasn't tall, but his shoulders and arms were packed with bulging muscles. He liked nothing better than to show off their strength, but not in a spot like this. He was wide of shoulder and deep of chest, and Wiley knew how powerful he was. He had seen him lift the rear end of a loaded wagon and hold it for several moments when two men couldn't budge it.

The sun couldn't tan Shannon's red face. Wiley couldn't remember a time when Shannon wasn't peeling. He had a snake-quick temper, and it was showing now. His smoky blue eyes were shooting flames at being sent out here.

The first attempt showed no coordination. Men heaved against each other, and their footing slipped. They could spend the rest of the year like this and never get the caisson out.

"Goddam it," Wiley raged. "Get together."

It went a little better. The caisson wheel lifted out of its miring with a sucking sound, then settled back.

Wiley straightened for a breath. It didn't take much concentrated effort like this to put an aching in a man's back. He raised a hand and wiped his dripping face, and he couldn't tell how much of it was caused by the water and how much by sweating.

Elam was closest to Shannon, and Shannon took out his mean temper on him.

"Get your back into it, Elam. Or we'll be out here all night."

Elam turned his head and looked at him, but he didn't respond.

Elam had been trying; Wiley could see the trembling that the effort had put into him.

"Leave him alone, Shannon," he said brusquely.

Shannon transferred those hot eyes to him. Wiley didn't want that attention on him, but it took it off Elam.

"Let's try it again," he said to divert Shannon's interest. "Now." They put another concentrated heave behind the wheels.

The sucking sound was more prolonged, and the wheels lifted and rolled half of their diameter toward harder ground. If they could have kept up the effort, they might have rolled it all the way, but all of the starch went out of their muscles. Only Shannon could have kept it up, but he couldn't do it alone.

"Come on, come on," he raved.

It didn't matter how much he raved, they had to wait until their pumping lungs eased.

Elam was in far worse shape, for his breathing

came in ragged gulps, and the trembling in his muscles had turned into an obvious shaking.

Wiley didn't know whether Elam lost his footing, or whether the shaking weakened him until he fell. He staggered backward and bumped hard into Shannon.

Shannon tried to shove him away and step back at the same time. His feet slipped from under him, and he sat down in the muddy water.

He stared up at Elam, and Wiley had seen that wild look before, almost a killing look. He tried to get around the caisson and step in between them, and he knew he was going to be too late.

Shannon heaved himself to his feet, fanning out a spray of water all around him. Elam watched him with a sort of horror frozen on his face. He lifted his hands in pleading, and the gesture had nothing defensive in it.

Shannon took a step and swung his heavy fist. It smashed Elam in the face, and a gagged coughing and a groan combined into a single sound. It was a brutal blow, and it yanked Elam out of the mud and sent him flying backward.

Wiley got a glimpse of Elam's face before his head disappeared beneath the surface. It had a blank slackness, and the eyes looked like pieces of glass. Elam was out.

"Get him out, get him out," he yelled as he plowed toward Shannon. He let his fist fly when he was still a long reach away, but he hadn't misjudged his distance. He clubbed Shannon on the back of the neck, putting the span of his shoulders behind it.

Even with the precarious footing, he got good leverage into the blow. Shannon's head flew forward, and the breath whooshed out of him. Shannon leaned lower as he made several staggering steps, trying to hold his balance. He did a fair job at that, for he was only beaten to his hands and knees, and he managed to keep his face from going under.

He turned a dazed look toward Wiley, and he made a visible effort to regain his scattered senses.

Wiley waded toward him. He reached Shannon just as the man straightened. He slammed his knee into the rising chin, and it made contact at its apex. It lifted Shannon a little higher and spilled him over backward. Wiley knew a tremendous satisfaction as Shannon's face went under water. That paid Shannon back for Elam.

The sustaining effort was all gone out of him, and he felt the weariness pull at his legs. Two men had Elam up on his feet, and the water must have revived him, for he kept shaking his head. Two others were pawing in the water to locate Shannon, and Wiley hoped they never found him.

"Get out of there," Buckley roared, and his face was a thundercloud. "Damn you, Anderson. Do you get in a fight everywhere you go?"

Wiley could have answered that it hadn't been

much of a fight, but he kept his mouth shut. Buckley had seen what had happened. If he put the wrong view on it, Wiley couldn't do anything about it.

"Report to Doniphan." Buckley's face was vicious. "I hope he gives you forty hours."

Wiley grimaced as he walked ahead of him. His boots squished with every step, and he was afraid his clinging socks were rubbing raw the tender skin on his toes. He looked like hell in this uniform before. How was he going to look in it after it dried?

Doniphan wasn't in his tent, and they waited a good fifteen minutes before he came in. Wiley thought there was a flicker of a smile in Doniphan's eyes, but his face was sober enough.

"What is it this time, Buckley?" Doniphan asked.

"Another fight, sir. He started one on a detail that was trying to pull a bogged caisson out. He kneed Shannon in the face and about tore his head off."

Wiley's eyes flamed. Not a word about Shannon knocking Elam cold. "That's a damned lie," Wiley yelped. "Shannon hit Elam first. I thought Elam was going to drown. I . . ."

Doniphan cut him off. "I saw it, Wiley. Buckley, your first concern was putting Wiley under charges, wasn't it? You didn't think that two men might drown."

Buckley's face flooded with color. "Sir, I . . ."

"I stayed to see that caisson out, Sergeant. Tell Shannon to report to me."

Buckley saluted and started to wheel around. Doniphan stopped him. "Sergeant, are you going to make a lifetime career out of finding Wiley in trouble?"

It was a subtle question, but Buckley understood it. His face burned, and he snapped, "No, sir." His tone gave the lie to his words.

Doniphan shook his head at Wiley as Buckley left the tent. "You handled it all right, Wiley. And those men worked pretty good for you. Until Shannon hit Elam. How would you like to be a corporal?"

Wiley didn't even take time to consider it. "No, sir. I'm not cut out for this kind of life."

Doniphan sighed. "I wish I could get at what's in your head, Wiley."

Whatever else he wanted to say was stopped by Shannon's entrance. Shannon was wet and bedraggled, and his eyes were murderous as he put them on Wiley. He didn't even look at Doniphan as he asked, "Did you send for me?"

Doniphan's jaw hardened. "Shannon, I saw it all happen. From beginning to end. Stay away from Anderson. If anything happens to him, I'll blame you for it. Do you understand that?"

Shannon's cheeks swelled with his repressed breath. He understood well enough.

"Did you hear me?" Doniphan snapped. At Shannon's sullen nod he said, "That's all."

He waited until Shannon left the tent. "I wish you would reconsider, Wiley."

He sighed as Wiley's lips firmed. That was answer enough. "At least I can give you something to look forward to, Wiley. We'll reach Bent's Fort on the Arkansas River in a few days. We'll stop there for two or three days to rest."

The word "river" rang big in Wiley's mind. It meant more water than a man had seen for a long time; it meant enough water to bathe and wash his clothes.

"Is that all, Aleck?"

"That's all, Wiley."

Wiley wished he could tell Doniphan what was troubling him; he wished he could ask his advice. But he knew what that advice would be, and he couldn't take it.

He grinned as he saluted. He had come out of this better than he had thought he would. "Thank you, Aleck."

He thought of Buckley and Shannon as he walked out of the tent. He had made good haters out of those two; each as deadly in his own as the other. He would have to watch them.

FOUR

Maria Yocupico crossed herself as she heard the pealing of the church bells. The comfort in them was gone, and in its place she felt a tremendous sadness. Once it had not been that way, and she could not say why it was so now, except that she could not help feeling that a bad time was ahead. Why did wars have to be? The United States had declared war on Mexico, and for the men it was a glorious time. They would crush the gringos and sweep them far back of the Rio Grande, yes, even out of Texas. The women did not see the glory; instead they saw the bloodshed, the killing, and the time of much grieving. She had lit many candles, praying the war would not come, but God had not listened to her. He had turned His face from His people, and though it might be questioning His wisdom, she could not understand why it had to be.

She put a mental curse on Governor Armijo. Hating him as she did might be a sin, but she could not help it. Armijo was a bad man with an authoritative foot on his people's necks. If the gringos won and sent Armijo fleeing, Maria doubted that they could be worse.

She looked around, and her face was guilty. She was glad that her thoughts could not be read and known. If Armijo knew of such things, his punishment would be quick and terrible. He was a vindictive man with an immense capacity for cruelty.

The sun reached her, and she moved back into the shade. She had waited over an hour outside the Palace of the Governors, as a dutiful sister should, and she was weary. But she would wait until Perea Yocupico came out of that building. She had not wanted him to go in there, but he hadn't listened to her. What business could he and the American have with Armijo?

Her brother was the only close living member of her family, and she loved him dearly. She had been very young when she had lost her mother, and her father had died a few years ago. It had made her and Perea close; until this war. Then he had closed his mind to her. She knew what he felt about Armijo, yet it looked as though he was trying to help him. He could easily offend him. Too many people had not come out of that building.

She could not repress a little scorn as two common women passed before her. The scorn died quickly. Aging came early to these women, and perhaps she should say a prayer to the Virgin Lady for the privileges she had been given. Her eighteen years had not yet touched her. She wore a dress of the finest silk, and she could not remember when she had gone without shoes. The women wore ragged dresses and were barefoot. Oh, her Lady would rebuke her severely for such thoughts. The cost of a pair of shoes could be a luxury beyond reach. Beauty wasn't distributed generously among these women. Too many faces were covered with smallpox pits, and their teeth were yellowed from the cornhusk cigarettes. It was an accepted thing that women smoked, and Maria had tried it. She had never got beyond the first, harsh, burning taste of them.

She moved another step. The band of shade, running along the base of the buildings, was getting thin. At this hour of the day the sun was pitiless in its searching out of any shade. Only the peasant women and a few Indians, in bright-colored blankets, were on Santa Fe's streets. And the merciless sun would drive them indoors before long. During the afternoon hours, Santa Fe would look like a deserted town, and activity wouldn't return to its streets until the sun sank.

Santa Fe sat on rolling sagebrush flats, and its buildings were made of adobe brick. A few of them had been plastered white but, primarily, it was a town of browns and grays. A creek ran out of the mountains, coursing south of the main part of town. Its deep, willow-choked ditch separated the scattering of houses south of it and the much more substantially built section on the north bank.

Stores and houses were built around the bare and sandy plaza, and the church occupied one corner of it. An effort had been made to beautify it, and a sundial was in the plaza's center. A few scrawny trees had been planted several years ago, but each year added to their losing battle with remorseless nature. The street running around the plaza always presented the obstacles of ruts. In times of moisture, the two-wheeled carretas cut deeply into the sand, and once the rains were over, the sun sculpted the grooves into an enduring hardness not to soften until the rains came again.

She was pressed against the building now. If Perea did not come out within a few minutes, she could not avoid the sun. She was a small thing, not reaching five feet tall, and her bones were fashioned on the same diminutive scale. Her hair was a shining black, held in order by a mother-of-pearl comb, then spilling loosely to below her shoulders. Her face was unmarked as yet by the stress of living. Her cheekbones were as delicately cut as a silversmith's work, and her enormous eyes were so dark brown that they looked black in certain lights. Her skin had a dusty translucence, and she was proud that her teeth were not yellowed. She was of quick temper, and she admitted it, but there were so many things that tried a person, particularly times like these. What was Perea doing that took so much time?

How well she knew the buildings around the

plaza! But she looked at them again to keep her attention occupied.

The Palace of Governors ran the entire north side of the plaza. A low tower was at each end, and the gallery across its front was supported every few feet by heavy posts. It was the heart of New Mexico's government, a massive, forbidding building, and she resisted the impulse to cross herself again. People said many dark things happened in it. Soldiers were stationed on guard along its length, and a few people trickled in and out of its doors.

La Fonda Inn was at the southwest corner, and it had an enormous main barroom. She had been in it once, though it was not a place a respectable woman visited. The Americans, while on their trading missions here, did much drinking and gambling there, and she had heard that a woman who went in there was only advertising what she was.

Her eyes went back to the Palace of Governors. Perea must be engaged in a lengthy business.

Myrick Dorsett sat across from Armijo's desk and watched him with alert eyes. Something was on Governor Armijo's mind, and he was trying to keep it well hidden. Perhaps he hadn't chosen too well in picking Perea Yocupico as a go-between. With the Mexicans, a man could never come right out and say what he thought. No, it must be a devious approach and retreat with all of the manners observed. So many hundreds of words had already been said, and he felt as though he was no closer to an agreement with Armijo than when they came in.

This chair was hard, and he wanted to slouch in it. He had never seen any Spanish furniture that was comfortable. He was a tall man with cold, chiseled features. The sun had darkened him so that, except for his height and blue eyes, he could have passed for one of the lighter Mexicans. He looked equally comfortable in a trader's stained hickory jacket or a blue fustian coat. He was in the blue now, and he smoked a long cigar. He had brought Armijo a big box of them, and Armijo had greedily snatched for it. This goddamned war had come too soon, and he wondered how Hendricks was making out. And what Armijo was going to do; that was the question.

Armijo looked like a small, swollen toad, sitting behind his desk. He was a fat man, and his face looked greasy with sweat. He was of poor background and breeding, but from somewhere he had had enough influence to get himself appointed to a position of great importance. As governor of New Mexico he represented Mexico, and his word was the final law. He had a low, cunning cupidity that was a grindstone, wearing the traders thin. He put an embargo on candle-wick, cotton drill, shoes, and cutlery. And those were just the big items. Anything that he figured was worth a tax was on the list.

Armijo pulled on his black mustache, and his eyes half-closed as he listened to Perea Yocupico's impassioned pleading. *Madre de Dios*! What did these two expect of him? That he pay for something that was not here?

A slow anger smoldered within him. He would let Yocupico go so far, then shut him up; for good if necessary. He walked softly with him, for Yocupico was from one of the finest families of Santa Fe. But if it was necessary, he would not hesitate to affront him.

"Don Perea, as I have pointed out, the rifles are not here."

Dorsett's voice was silky. "And as His Excellency knows, I explained where the rifles are." He writhed inwardly at the thought of those rifles in the wagons. He had expected Hendricks to have gotten them here several weeks ago, and the fool had gotten himself trapped in Kearny's march. His eyes glistened as he thought of the sum those rifles would bring. He had bankrupted himself to get his hands on them. Without them, Armijo was in no position to put up much of a defense. The majority of his army was made up of poorly trained barefoot peasants, and they were armed with swords, bows and arrows, and machetes. A few well-aimed shots would put them into wild flight. It had taken him time to set up this deal; it had taken time to find the man he could use. Yocupico was the right one, intensely patriotic and loving his Santa Fe and New Mexico. Yocupico had listened to Dorsett, then had agreed to approach Armijo. Armijo had wanted those rifles; he had been eager to dip into the tax money he had stolen for himself. But he would not show the color of his gold until he had those modern rifles in his hands. The problem of delivery was driving Dorsett wild. He wanted to turn the rifles over to Armijo and get Linda out of this country. She was languishing under this heat, and her loss of weight was noticeable. If Armijo would make a stand outside of Santa Fe, Hendricks could slip the wagons through in the chaos of the battle. Now a new rumor was disturbing Dorsett. Armijo wasn't going to make a defense. An American delegation had reached him and bought him out. Armijo was only waiting for the propitious moment to make his flight.

Was it true? Dorsett squirmed under the pressure of the question. Yocupico hadn't dared put the question into bare words. He had sparred and feinted, retreated and advanced. Now his patience was growing thin. It showed on his face.

Dorsett covertly watched him. How far did the man dare go? Yocupico was a small man, not standing over five-foot-six inches. His face was thinned by his passionate nature. He was dressed in the old style, ruffled Rouen shirt and green corduroy jacket. His black kid shoes were almost effeminate. But Dorsett didn't for a moment doubt his courage. It took courage to walk into Armijo's office and accuse him, even by implication.

"If we knew where you planned on your defense," Yocupico said, "we could get the wagons there."

Armijo yawned. "The talk grows tedious, Don Perea. I tell my plans only to my officers. And I will not buy the rifles until I see them."

"But if you are not here to buy them?" Yocupico purred.

Armijo's eyes glittered. "What are you saying?"

"That it is possible that you may make no defense of Santa Fe."

Armijo pounded the desk with his fist. "A damnable lie. Who says such things?"

Yocupico shook his head, disclaiming that any blame could be placed on him. "Only talk that is heard in the *cantinas*, Governor. That the gringos will pay you well to make no defense."

Armijo's face was livid with rage. "It is a lie. By the Mother of God, I swear it. When have I seen the gringos? When would I have talked with them?"

Yocupico shrugged, and the gesture said many things. Some of the traders were still in town; Armijo could have talked to the Americans many times.

"But you defend Santa Fe," Yocupico persisted.

Some inner turmoil increased Armijo's sweating. "I defend New Mexico in Apache Canyon. It is an impenetrable position." He glowered darkly at Yocupico, then at Dorsett. "Get the rifles to me there."

He stood abruptly and strode out of the room.

Dorsett looked at Yocupico, and a question was big in his eyes. But he was wise enough not to put it into words.

Yocupico smiled faintly. "I guess we go now, Señor."

Dorsett waited until they were outside. "Can he be trusted?"

Yocupico's shrug had a fatalistic quality. "*Quien sabe*? You heard what he said."

Dorsett chewed on his lower lip. He wished he knew what he should do. "I'll send somebody to get word to Hendricks. When Kearny's column gets near Apache Canyon, Hendricks will have to find a way to slip those wagons away."

Yocupico's face was beginning to show weariness. In something like this a man had to put so many devious qualities together, and then he couldn't be sure what he would have.

"It is your job, Señor." He could trust Dorsett to that extent; Dorsett wanted to sell those rifles. *Por Dios*, he thought with a sudden hopelessness. A country's future depended upon such men as Dorsett and Armijo. His eyes flashed with sudden decision. If Armijo did not buy those rifles, he, Don Perea Yocupico, would take them by force. He could raise enough patriots who felt as he did. Let the Americans win their first battle in New Mexico. The following revolution would sweep them out of New Mexico.

Dorsett kept putting side glances on him. What was Yocupico thinking? Dorsett could converse with these people, but he never knew what they were thinking. He would have to find somebody to deliver the news to Hendricks. It had to be a Mexican, he decided; somebody who knew the country well. He wouldn't dare send an American, even if he knew of one he could trust that much.

"Pardon me, Señor." Yocupico was looking across the street. "My sister is waiting for me."

He started away, and Dorsett checked him. Dorsett hated to lose contact with this man, even for a short while.

"I was hoping you and your sister would have dinner with me tonight." He had met Maria Yocupico once, though it had been a grudging introduction. And he had never been asked to the Yocupico hacienda.

"My excuses, Señor, but other things occupy us tonight."

Yocupico strode away without looking back. He was sure the gringo would watch him all the way across the plaza. His refusal had been curt enough to the point of rudeness, and he did not care.

"Why do you stand out here?" he asked Maria. His face was stern, but he could not hide the softness in his eyes.

"Because I worry, Perea. Each time you go into that building I do not know if you come out again or not."

Her concern pleased him, and he took her arm. "Do you fear the dragon in there that much? Do not worry your head. It went well."

He lengthened his stride. He wanted to get inside the cool, thick walls of his hacienda, he wanted to take a siesta. He wished he could believe his own words. He did not know whether or not it had gone well.

FIVE

Dorsett tapped lightly on the door before he opened it. His face was anxious as he entered the room in La Fonda. "Do you feel any better?"

Linda Anderson turned her head on the bed, and smiled at him. Her hair was dank with perspiration, and her color wasn't good.

"Yes." There was no conviction in the answer.

He always felt this wonder when he looked at her. He had known many women in his life but never the capacity to love one. With her, he had found it. He remembered the first time he had seen her, how difficult his breathing had seemed to be. She had fought leaving Wiley Anderson, but he had overcome that. He was sure she had never regretted it. His touch could still put a shining wetness in her eyes.

An errant breeze carried additional hot air into the room. He stepped to the window and closed it. He smiled at her. "You can't believe it's cooler with it closed."

"It's so hot in here, Myrick. And the room seems to grow smaller."

He knew what she meant. This was hellish country on her, and she spent too much time in here. These rooms weren't built for Anglo-Saxons. The ceiling was too low, and the walls always seemed to be bearing in on one.

"Where would you like to eat dinner tonight, Linda?"

She was indifferent to the prospect, and he could not blame her. All the meals were the same, and after a time they bore heavily on an American stomach. He, too, found no pleasure in the thought of another one. The choice had monotonous sameness; chili, tamales, or mutton, and all of it too hot with spices.

He sat down on the edge of the bed and took one of her hands. "You've got to eat something, Linda." He bent over and brushed her forehead with his lips. "We won't be here much longer."

That put a little brightness in her eyes. He pushed the blonde hair from her cheeks. It had lost its shining luster, and her blue eyes were dull. She was still a beautiful woman, though not as she had looked when she left Missouri.

She would look that way again, he determined. With a cooler climate and new clothes, she would be a different woman. Once Hendricks got through, Dorsett would have enough money to take her anyplace, and he bubbled with hope at the thought.

"How would you like to go to San Francisco, Linda? Or even to Paris?" The enthusiasm of it fired him. If he could collect Armijo's money, the world would belong to them.

"I would like that, Myrick."

She had brightened noticeably, and he nodded

with approval. "And you'll try to eat tonight."

"I'll try."

He strode about the room with brisk strides. Just seeing her response was a tonic to him. "I have to find Rufino Rocha, Linda. It shouldn't take me long. I have an errand for him to do."

She nodded with indifference. She knew Rocha, but she had no interest in him; perhaps it was because they couldn't exchange a dozen words between them. She knew that Rocha was available if she wanted some chore performed, and that was enough for her.

He picked up a piece of paper and a pencil and thrust them into his pocket. Rocha wouldn't be able to speak to Hendricks, either. Dorsett thought about writing the note here and decided against it. Its composition wasn't yet clear in his mind.

"I won't be long," he promised from the door.

Rocha lived in a doorless house in the poorer part of the town. Dorsett hesitated in the doorway, adjusting his eyes to the darkness of the room after the brilliance of the sun outside. The sound of Rocha's snoring carried to him.

Rocha was lying on a pallet on the earthen floor, and his upper body was bathed in sweat. Flies buzzed about his face, or crawled on his bare chest, but they didn't bother him enough to break the rhythm of his snoring. The room was stifling, and Dorsett didn't see how Rocha stood it. This was a dreary, shabby room, the plaster crumbling from the walls and exposing the adobe bricks. Rocha was womanless, and the room showed it. The floor hadn't been swept in a long time, and the few pieces of furniture were sagging, or broken and covered with a thick film of dust.

Dorsett had hired Rocha before, and the man knew him and Hendricks well, and looked forward to their occasional trading trips. Betweentimes, he existed by collecting firewood along the creek. Dorsett didn't know how Rocha made his living. The half-dozen goats in the falling-down pen back of the house couldn't bring in enough of an income to keep a man. He hadn't seen them this time, but he knew they were out there. Their smell filled the room.

He reached down and shook Rocha awake. Rocha came to sluggishly, yawning and rubbing at his eyes. He sat up, and his chest was scrawny and stringy. Dorsett didn't know how old he was, somewhere in his early sixties, he supposed. He hadn't used him on this trip, but he had a use for him now. He could trust Rocha to do exactly as he was told. Rocha knew the country well, and the Americans wouldn't think of stopping an old Mexican on some aimless trip through the countryside.

"Rufino, I have a job for you." Dorsett spoke in Spanish, for Rocha knew only a few words of

English. It was better that he did not speak nor understand it.

Eagerness moved the deep wrinkles into a happy grin and exposed the gaps of his gums. "*Si*, Señor. I will do anything for you."

Dorsett's face was set stern to express the seriousness of this. "You will tell nobody where you go, or whom you see. Do you understand?"

"*Si, si.*"

"I will give you a note to carry to Hendricks. You remember Señor Hendricks?"

"I remember him well." Hendricks was another generous American. "Where do I find him?"

"The report is that the American army has entered New Mexico. The traders' wagons are following it. Hendricks will be behind General Kearny's army somewhere on the road to Santa Fe."

Rocha's apprehensiveness showed on his face. "Señor, you want me to go through the gringo army? They will stop me."

Dorsett made an impatient gesture. "Damn it, Rufino. Use your head. You will go around the army until you find the traders' camp. Give the note to nobody else but Hendricks. Is that clear?"

He questioned Rocha several times until he was certain Rocha understood everything. Now he would offer him a sum of money that would make Rocha forget all of his fears.

"Fifty dollars, American money, if you deliver

my note to Hendricks. Twenty-five dollars before you go; twenty-five when you return and tell me the note was delivered."

Rocha's mouth sagged and his eyes bulged. He had never had that much money at one time in his hands, and had never expected that he would. Tears watered his eyes at the thought of what so much money could buy him.

Dorsett watched him with sour satisfaction. If Rocha accomplished this simple task, it would go well. It could hinge on Armijo making his stand at Apache Canyon, but the governor had to make his stand someplace. Of course Armijo could flee as rumor had it, but there always were the imponderables Dorsett couldn't figure. Once the battle was joined, Hendricks could slip the wagons away. During the battle, Kearny would have no time nor men to keep eyes on Hendricks. Dorsett had gone over it a dozen times in his head. He saw flaws, too many of them, but he could do nothing about it. He had to make the best plans he could and be prepared to change them with the course of events.

He scowled at the paper before he wrote, "Will be at Apache Canyon." He left the short note unsigned. Hendricks would know his writing. Hendricks would be alerted to keep on the watch for him. He tore the edges of the paper away so that only the single line remained when he handed it to Rocha.

"Get this to him, Rufino. Nobody else. And get back here as fast as you can."

A thought struck him. What if Rocha was captured and the note found on him? Rocha would not be able to explain it, but it still might have meaning to unfriendly eyes.

"If you can't get it through to him, eat this paper, Rufino. I mean that."

The apprehension returned to Rocha's eyes as he looked at the scrap of paper. "Eat it, Señor?" At the awful frown on Dorsett's face he said hastily, "Eat it, Señor. I understand."

SIX

Kearny's column wound through the mountainous country of New Mexico. While the sun was as fierce as ever, the air was drier, and a man didn't suffer so much. Wiley felt better than he had all the way across Kansas. He wasn't sweating, like he had before, and the sun seemed to have burned the last remnant of the fever out of his system. It was a strange country, filled with sand, creosote and greasewood bushes, and ringed about with mountains that turned red under a sunset. He kept wondering how a man made a living in a land this hostile.

They were in the middle of August, and he had seen his first Mexicans. They were little, brown people with shy, almost frightened eyes. They peered out of the brush, their faces showing readiness to take flight. They reminded Wiley of the squirrels he had hunted in Missouri. Those little animals had peered down at him through the leafy branches when they thought they were unseen.

Eight feet tall, he thought. All that talk was damned lies. These Mexicans just didn't look to be cut out as fighters. If he guessed right, all these people wanted was to be left alone on their poor land. This land didn't appear to give them much. Their clothes were mostly of some cheap white cotton cloth, and their wide, high straws were floppy and broken. Sombreros, Elam called them. Hell, most of them couldn't even afford shoes or boots.

Even if they showed willingness for it, he hadn't come here to fight. He was in New Mexico, and Santa Fe was ahead, a short distance compared to the miles they had traveled. His anticipation quickened his blood. It wouldn't be long before he found Linda.

He kept watching ahead with wary eyes. Armijo had sent formal notification that the Mexican army would resist at Begas, nine miles ahead. Wiley might have to fight there to get through to Santa Fe.

A man was left limp when the keying up was gone. Kearny's scouts found no enemy at Begas. Kearny had to stop to make a speech to the inhabitants, announcing that New Mexico was now claimed by the United States.

Wiley sat in the mounted ranks and listened sourly. Kearny made a windy speech, and there was no applause at its end. He doubted that any of these people could understand a word.

Kearny ordered the march continued, and Doniphan passed close to Wiley. Wiley shook up the claybank to catch up with him.

"Do you think Armijo ran for good, Aleck?"

Doniphan shook his head. "We have a new report now, Wiley. Armijo will make his stand at a pass a couple of miles ahead. Keep your eyes on Kearny. You'll see him put the army in the line of battle; his regulars ahead, the Missouri volunteers following." His smile was pained. "Kearny still doesn't trust us."

Wiley found no fault in that. Let the regulars go ahead any time they wanted. He talked it over with Elam, and that was excitement shining in his face, not fear. Wiley glared at him. Couldn't Elam realize they might be going into a battle? He remembered the little brown people, and his tension eased. It couldn't be much of a battle.

He judged they had gone over a mile when Kearny put the army into a line of battle. The tension came back, and he felt the sweating break out afresh on him. Every man was issued ten cartridges apiece, and the cavalrymen tied their sabers to their wrists with their kerchiefs. The infantry battalion fixed their bayonets and scaled the high, steep rocky eminence to flank the gap ahead. At the bugle, the dragoons moved ahead at a trot, leading the Missouri regiment.

A thin blue line fanned out as it moved on the gap. Wiley took a paper cartridge from his cartridge box and opened the breech of his Jenks. The cartridge held a ball and measure of powder, and he jammed it home in the breech. Bugles were sounding all over the place, and men, carrying muzzle loaders, had to hold the muzzles up to keep the ball from rolling out.

Wiley wondered how much of his sweating was exertion and how much worry. His flesh was tensed as he waited for the report of the first shot, and it never came. He still couldn't believe it even after they had passed through the gap. Armijo was nowhere within sight.

Wiley swallowed hard. Everybody had that blank, astonished look. They had built up for a climax, and the letdown was jarring.

Kearny marched them sixteen miles and camped near the Mexican settlement near San Miguel Springs. The springs eased the water problem, though the details were as numerous as ever. Bent's Fort was over two hundred miles behind them, and Wiley remembered the three days they had spent there with appreciation. Those days had been a pleasant relaxation in the marching. If it weren't for his driving purpose, he would have been glad to spend the rest of the campaign there.

He talked it over with Elam as they rubbed down their horses. Regulations weren't the sole reason Wiley performed it daily. It had helped get the claybank this far in good shape. Too many men ducked the chore whenever they could. That was all right with Wiley. Let their horses get the gall sores.

"What do you think about today?" he asked Elam.

"I've heard a lot of grumbling, Wiley. Some of

the men say it was only a practice run, set up by Kearny. Maybe it's true; maybe he wanted to get a look at how we looked."

Wiley remembered his tension. He felt like grumbling too. That was asking a lot of a man.

He had his half shelter off the company wagon and erected, and his equipment was polished. He was lucky enough to draw no wood detail or sentry duty. The rest of the time until taps was his.

"What are we going to do tonight?" Elam asked.

Wiley didn't have a wide choice. He could read, or write a letter until the fading light made it useless. He could get into a card game that always sprang up along the tent rows, but none of those things interested him.

"I'm just going to look around a little." He hoped the vagueness of the answer would discourage Elam.

It apparently did, for Elam started to turn away. "I guess I'd better get a letter written."

Wiley took his rifle with him. He would rather have taken a pistol as being less obvious, but he didn't have one. The rifle shouldn't keep him from being able to slip by the sentries. He would catch it from both sides if he was caught out there. He was in enemy country.

After today's fiasco, the thought of enemies didn't worry him too much. There hadn't been the smell of one ever since they had entered New Mexico. He had slipped by the sentries every night since Kearny led them here. He didn't know for sure what he expected, but he hoped to see Dorsett trying to get into the traders' camp. He set his teeth. If only he could be that lucky!

Darkness came quickly for there was no twilight in this country. It felt strange after the long summer evenings in Missouri. He worked his way as close as he dared to the traders' camp, close enough to make out details on the dark figures passing between him and the cooking fires.

He picked a high elevation, just outside of Hendricks' wagons, and he settled down. This was probably foolishness, he accused himself. What would he do, if he did see Dorsett here? He couldn't take him all by himself. Maybe he should have told Elam about it, but Elam wouldn't have appreciated all those wasted nights, unless Wiley told him why. And he couldn't bring himself to talk about Linda.

The sand was still hot from the day's sun, and an occasional strong breeze rustled it. If a man lay here long enough, he could get to imagining that the sand talked in tiny voices.

He tightened as he thought he heard a crawling, scraping sound. What kind of nocturnal animals were about in the night? Were they dangerous? He had heard that rattlesnakes abounded, and he broke out in cold sweating. Nobody could say that rattlesnakes weren't dangerous.

The sound persisted, and he saw what made it. For an instant, his tightly strung imagination magnified it larger than its actual size, and he half-set the rifle butt to his shoulder.

He lowered it as he saw the figure making its careful way from bush to bush. It was going to pass not ten feet from him, and his eyes blazed. It had happened; Dorsett was here.

He raised to his hands and knees, then got his feet under him, crouching low. The figure was moving at a slight tangent from him, and it didn't have the slightest notion Wiley was around. A bitter disappointment flooded him. That wasn't Dorsett. It was much smaller. Its stealth suggested a hidden purpose, and a thought struck Wiley. Maybe Dorsett had sent it on some errand. He could let it go, or capture it to learn its purpose.

He straightened and made three long, soundless strides before the man turned his head. Wiley was close enough to see the mouth sag and fear spread across his face.

It was one of the little brown people, and Wiley wanted to swear at him. "You move and I'll blow your head off." Maybe the man couldn't understand what he said. He threatened him with the rifle muzzle. The Mexican could understand that.

The man's hands raised pleadingly, and his

voice was a faint gasp. "*Por favor*, Señor."

Wiley was in the same boat, for those words didn't mean anything to him. "What are you doing out here?" Before the question slipped out, he knew it was useless. He pointed toward the traders' camp. "Is that where you're going?"

The man violently shook his head. He made a sudden grab for a pocket, and if it hadn't been the shirt pocket, Wiley would have shot him.

The hand flashed into the pocket and out, then popped into his mouth. Wiley wasn't close enough to see it plainly, but he could swear that was a piece of paper.

He sprang forward and seized the wrist with his left hand. The man struggled briefly with a burst of energy that didn't last, and Wiley saw that he was old. He pulled the hand away from the mouth and thought he heard teeth click in a violent chewing motion. The Adam's apple ran up and down, then the swallowing was over. Whatever had been in the man's mouth was gone.

Wiley didn't know what this was all about, but he had better take him to somebody who could figure it out. He spun him until he faced in the direction of the army camp. He put the muzzle of the rifle in the small of the back and shoved. The man didn't need any words; he had been given enough signs to understand.

He moved ahead of Wiley with shambling

steps, every now and then turning a pleading face over his shoulder. Wiley only shoved him a little harder.

A sentry challenged Wiley, and it was one of the Missouri Volunteers. Wiley sighed. That made it easier. He wanted to take his man to Doniphan and not Kearny or some of the other officers. Sometimes a regular was damned difficult to deal with.

"Simons," he said. "It's Wiley Anderson. I found this Mexican out in the brush. I think Doniphan ought to talk to him."

Simons was a lanky farm boy with long arms and legs that didn't quite seem to coordinate with him. His eyes ran curiously over the Mexican. "What do you think he was doing out there, Wiley?"

Wiley made a show of bristling. He wasn't going to take time to try to explain something to Simons that he didn't understand himself. "Doniphan will skin you, if you don't let me through."

Simons felt so too, but he wanted to be in on part of it. "I'll take you in."

"You better hadn't. If they find you away from your post, they'll call it desertion in the face of the enemy."

Simons scratched his jaw with a thumbnail. "Hell, he don't look like no enemy." He stepped out of Wiley's way. "But I guess you're right."

Wiley pushed the Mexican past Simons. He wanted to get the man to Doniphan without arousing too much interest. The wish wasn't granted. He had a half-dozen men following him when he reached Doniphan's tent. But that could have been expected. Nobody could shove a Mexican down the company street without arousing attention.

He glared at them before he shoved the Mexican inside the tent. "Don't none of you try to follow us."

Doniphan was alone, and if he felt surprise, it didn't show. "What have you got, Wiley?"

"A Mexican, Aleck. I found him sulking out in the brush."

Doniphan's eyes sharpened. "You think he was there to spy out our camp?"

"I did at first. But he wasn't even headed in that direction. He'd already passed our camp. He was trying to get into the traders' camp."

Doniphan frowned as he studied the Mexican. "Maybe he was lost. What did he want in the traders' camp?"

Wiley wished he knew. "He couldn't understand me, and I didn't understand him." He glanced at the Mexican. Wiley's rifle wasn't on him, but the man still trembled. "Look at him. I musta scared the shit out of him. I don't think he was just stumbling around in the brush. He knew where he was going."

Doniphan brushed the man with his eyes. "What makes you think that?"

"Before I could grab him he stuffed something in his mouth. Maybe I can't swear to it, but it looked like a scrap of paper. He swallowed it before I could stop him."

Doniphan leaned forward, his eyes intent. "You think he was trying to get information to somebody in the traders' camp?"

"It looks that way." Wiley was afraid Doniphan was going to ask the next logical question, and he forestalled it. "I don't know who he wanted to see." He thought he had made a bad mistake out there. He should have tried to trail the Mexican into the traders' camp and see which one he contacted. But it was too late to think of that now.

Doniphan stood with a tired sigh. "Maybe he's as harmless as he appears to be, Wiley. But I'd better take him to Kearny. Surely he's got somebody around who can talk a little Spanish."

"Do I have to go along to guard him?"

Doniphan smiled. "I think I can handle him. Maybe it's best you not go along. Kearny would want to know how you happened to be in the path of this man."

Stubbornness hardened Wiley's face. Only his personal business would explain it, and he wasn't about to talk about it.

Doniphan's face was regretful. "Go along, Wiley. I'll see what I can find out about him."

Wiley turned and stepped outside the tent. Several of the troopers had lingered, and they crowded about him, wanting information. They hadn't dared press too close to Doniphan's tent, and now they pulled at him for talk. They patted him on the back, they praised his nerve in capturing a dangerous Mexican enemy.

Wiley snorted at the memory of an old, frightened Mexican. "You guys are crazy as hell," he said and stalked away from them.

He didn't get a chance to see Doniphan until the following morning. "We found somebody to talk to him, Wiley. He would give his name and that's about all. Rufino Rocha."

Wiley put the strange-sounding name in his mind. "Why was he going to the traders' camp?"

"He wouldn't say. He would hardly say a word."

"What did you do with him?"

"Kearny intends to keep him until we get to Apache Canyon. The latest reports say Armijo has built fortifications there. Kearny doesn't want to give Rocha a chance to do us harm."

Wiley thought about Rufino Rocha as he rode toward Apache Canyon. He had little or nothing to base it on, but he felt Rocha had no connection with the Mexican military. It kept Wiley's mind so occupied that he hardly thought of the imminent battle at Apache Canyon.

The companies of mounted and foot wheeled and maneuvered into line of battle with not quite the degree of bumbling as the first time. Maybe Kearny's practice run had made for a little smoothness. Ammunition was issued, and rifles were loaded. Sabers were tied to wrists, and the dragoons led the way at a slow, cautious walk. It picked up to a trot, then into a wild run. They were chasing the wind. Armijo had been here, and he had made his preparations. Kearny's army found redoubts and felled timber bastions, but no Mexicans. Armijo had been here all right, but something had happened to change his mind.

Elam spat into the sand and untied his saber from his wrist. "Armijo ran again, Wiley."

Wiley grinned. "I hope it gets to be a lasting habit." Where would Armijo stop next? Las Vegas? Or would he hold back all his efforts until Santa Fe? After they reached Santa Fe, none of this conjecture would bother him again. Let the army hunt for Armijo. He had his own personal search to occupy him.

SEVEN

The little brown people seemed, for the most part, friendly. Every time Kearny's army approached one of the small villages, the people were clustered outside it, bowing and scraping, their sombreros clutched to their chests.

"Hell, they don't want to fight," Wiley said. It suited him just fine. He heard several of the troopers make sneering remarks about the courage of these people. These remarks had increased ever since they had found Apache Canyon empty. He didn't give them much weight. A man could talk pretty big when the threat of a battle was taken away.

These people ardently craved peace; it was in their cringing, in their hopeful faces. Wiley found himself grinning at them, and they returned it. He had spent a lot of hours worrying about fighting these people. They were wasted hours, for he couldn't see any danger in them at all.

Reports drifted down through the officers, and each man passing them on distorted them a little more. The last one Wiley had heard said that Armijo had fled Mexico with only his personal retinue of dragoons. The troopers made ribald jokes about Armijo's cowardice, but it suited

Wiley just fine. He had no personal score to settle with Armijo.

He grinned at Elam. "Daniel, did you hear all of that big talk? Every man here has followed Kearny for the sole pleasure of whipping the entire Mexican army all by himself."

"I wasn't counting myself in on that," Elam said dryly. "What's the last amount you heard Armijo collected to get out of New Mexico?"

"The first was fifty thousand dollars, then it kept growing. The last I heard was over a hundred thousand. Every man adds some more to it. We must have the damndest collection of liars ever put together."

Elam smiled. "That's human nature, Wiley. Each man adds to it."

"Is any of it truth?" Wiley growled. "Do you think the United States paid him anything?"

"I think it's possible. If the diplomats handled it, we'll never get at the truth. They're a sneaky bunch. But if the United States did buy Armijo off, even at a cost of fifty thousand dollars, it would be a cheap price to pay for New Mexico. But are the diplomats sure that Armijo is the only one who will defend it?"

Wiley spat into the sand. "It's one of those deals that smells like it was made in an outhouse. If Armijo got that money, he won't divide it with anybody, will he?"

Elam laughed. "You can bet he won't. Mexico's

leaders have done this sort of thing before." He squinted at Wiley. "Something's picking at you."

"I'm thinking of the little people Armijo deserted. I don't blame them for not wanting to fight for something Armijo didn't think worth defending."

Elam nodded approval. "You thought that through pretty good. But you've overlooked something. What class are those people who gather to watch us in?"

Wiley gave him a puzzled frown. Those people all looked alike to him.

"We're seeing only the poor people, the peasants. It's not over yet as easy as you make it sound, Wiley. The poor people don't make the wars. They're too busy trying to make a living. Have you seen a well-dressed person among them?" He smiled as Wiley shook his head. "I thought not. The poor peasants don't understand what makes wars and why they're shoved into them. Right now, they think we're winning. They're trying to show us how happy they are about it. But where are the rich-dressed ones? The leaders, the makers of war, come out of that class."

Wiley scowled at him. Elam could ask questions that crammed a man's head and beat on it for exit. He couldn't recall a Mexican who belonged to the upper class. The upper-class Mexicans hadn't accepted the Americans. Damn Elam. He pointed out a few things, and something that seemed so simple was suddenly complex. Elam didn't think the war was over.

"Daniel, you put that crawling back between my shoulders. You think this war's got a long way to go?"

"I think it'll be some time before we're welcomed here," Elam said dryly.

Wiley's face was gloomy as he stared down the road. Why did he give a damn how much longer it lasted? His part in it would be short-lived.

The Santa Fe trail had wound monotonously before them. It had twisted and dipped, then risen again. It led out of Las Vegas south to the foothills. The mountains rose again, and the Raton Pass was a deep red slash. The dwarfed piñons were in the higher reaches, and the grama grass didn't look strong enough to feed a hungry cow.

He had to admit he would miss some phases of this war. He would certainly miss Daniel Elam. The close association had enriched their relations. He could add some others to his list of likings, and he admitted he felt physically better than he had in a long time. The daily routine that used to grind him up so thoroughly was no longer unbearable. His endurance had increased as his muscles hardened, and his breathing was clearer than it had been in a long time. He had started out with a hating for this country and all it meant, and, he thought wryly, he had received something good in return.

Still, he would never pick it to live in for the rest of his life. Its vegetation was poor and sparse, the land seeming mostly sand. It was all high country. It seemed that every place a man looked, he saw cliffs standing vertically, or leaning tilted, threatening to come rolling down on a man's head.

It would be hell on horses and women, he thought. He had put additional care on his horse to get it through in decent shape, and some of the cavalrymen were now walking because of their carelessness. He had seen this country's harsh etching in women's faces, making them look years older than they were. He shook his head. A man could kind of claw his way through it, but a woman didn't have that kind of inbuilt toughness.

This land had no outstanding colors that caught an eye. It was mostly browns and reds, mixed with splashes of yellows. All of the colors were subdued, mostly drab when the daylight was full. But when the sun caught them at the right angle, particularly at morning and evening, the blended result caught up a man's breath.

He wondered what the plants were that so profusely dotted the canyon side. It seemed impossible that a plant could find enough soil to root in on those steep sides. Every plant he saw in New Mexico seemed thorny or spiky, and this plant was no different. It had long spiky leaves, bunched in the middle, then reaching out their spiny length. Stalks of white, waxy flowers lifted quite high, some of them coming up to a man on horseback.

"Daniel, do you know what those flowers are?"

Elam said something in Spanish, then seeing that Wiley didn't understand, translated it for him. "The candles of our Lord."

It was a rare piece of beauty in a harsh country, and Wiley stared at them. "They're right pretty, Daniel. It sounded pretty in Spanish too."

Elam nodded. "The Spanish language is beautiful, Wiley."

Wiley couldn't argue about that. His attention was caught by activity ahead of them.

The canyon was broadening out, and they must be getting close to its mouth. Men and horses up ahead seemed to be moving with a new haste, and an odd eagerness seemed to be transmitting itself up and down the column.

Elam gave his horse more rein. "Maybe the vanguard has sighted Santa Fe. I heard an officer in the Topographical Corps say last night that we would see Santa Fe today."

Wiley stood in the stirrups. He couldn't see a damned thing up ahead. But there was a definite picking up in the column's speed. Santa Fe was the capital of New Mexico, and it was the army's goal. Wiley felt that same eagerness run through him. If that was Santa Fe up ahead, he wanted to get a look at it too. He expected more than the sorry mud villages they had passed through.

The canyon floor was strewn with boulders, but it didn't put any caution in the artillerymen. Wiley scowled as a battery came clattering through, forcing its passage through the traffic. The caisson wheels took a pounding against those rocks. It was a wonder that wheels lasted as long as they did. Wiley threw a curse after the artillerymen. If they broke one of those caissons, it would be other troopers who had to help them get out of trouble.

"I wonder how far we've come, Daniel."

"I was curious enough to ask. Eight hundred and ten miles on the viameter on the Topographical wagon. That was last night. I'm guessing we covered ten more today. That would make it about eight hundred and twenty miles, if that's Santa Fe up ahead."

Wiley shook his head. He would have called any man a liar, if he had predicted he would take a trip this long. "It's a hell of a way," he grumbled. "Santa Fe better be worth seeing."

The column widened as it came out of the canyon and poured over the sloping sagebrush flats. Santa Fe seemed only a little distance ahead, though Wiley had learned how deceiving distance was in mountainous country.

He pulled the claybank to a halt, staring at the

collection of buildings ahead. In the clear air they stood out plain and distinct, every detail of them standing out sharply. He felt an unreasonable anger as though he had been cheated, and couldn't explain how or why. This was no different from the other villages he had passed through; bigger but no better. He felt gloomy and depressed, and he couldn't put his finger on that either. Were Dorsett and Linda in Santa Fe? He couldn't answer that until he searched it. Did he know what he was going to do about her? He couldn't answer that, either, until he saw her.

Something struck him with cruel irony. What if the Mexicans put up their first defense just outside of Santa Fe? What if he had to fight his way clear through the damned Mexican army just to ride into that depressing mud town?

EIGHT

The Mexicans made no defense of Santa Fe, and that didn't lean Wiley toward the city's favor. The closer he drew to it, the less he was impressed with it.

"Daniel, who would build their houses out of mud bricks?"

"People who have no other kind of material," Elam rebuked him. "How much timber have you seen around here that would make decent lumber?"

Wiley had the grace to turn red. "I hadn't thought of that."

"Adobe bricks of sun-hardened mud, Wiley. I've read they make a very satisfactory house. Cool in the summer and warm in the winter."

"I still wouldn't trade them," Wiley growled.

He couldn't keep it hidden, but the closer they came to Santa Fe, the higher his interest mounted. A creek split it, and this town was laid out in square lines, each building adding white, or tan, or gray to the picture. Wiley thought the creek wasn't much as they crossed it, but it had steep, deep banks. Sometime in the past, a heavy wash of water had cut through this sandy soil.

Santa Fe wasn't built for an army to ride into. Kearny had to break the column of fours into a column of twos to get through the narrow streets. Pedestrians using a street at the same time as the army, did so in peril of their lives and bones. They had to throw themselves against a building wall and press tightly, for the column was at a gallop. The wagons clattered after, adding to the din. Kearny wanted to impress Santa Fe, Wiley thought sourly. It seemed like a quick and sure way to put a sour taste in the Mexicans' mouths.

The column poured out into the plaza, and Kearny's upflung hand stopped it.

Wiley groaned as he guessed at Kearny's intentions. "He's not holding another ceremony like he did at Las Vegas?"

Elam grinned at Wiley's unhappiness. "Don't you know a general never misses an opportunity like this?"

Wiley's butt would know it. He remembered how it had ached after sitting at attention in Las Vegas.

Kearny and his staff were on the roof of the long building on the north side of the square. The infantry were at parade rest, and six companies of dragoons sat in precise ranks before them. Somewhere the officers had found an opportunity to make a quick change, for they wore their yellow-and-white silk sashes and white-plumed dress helmets.

Wiley had heard that Kearny's fever had returned since leaving Las Vegas, and he showed it. His face was almost a match for his sash.

Major Clark had his two batteries on a low hill above the town. Wiley wondered what the thirteen-gun salute was for. Its rolling booms echoed over the town, and Wiley wondered if it impressed the Mexicans enough to make up for the waste of powder.

Kearny was well into his speech, and he was repeating the Las Vegas one. Wiley heard the phrase, "possession of New Mexico peacefully in the United State's name," and let his mind wander. He could move his eyes and little else without being caught. That sandy plaza in front of him was a sorry thing. No chairs or benches or anything else for comfort. The sundial sure didn't do much to make it prettier, and the scrawny trees would take a long time to grow enough to put out any shade.

Kearny droned on, pausing every sentence or two so that a Mexican could translate it into Spanish. "We have marched here, hoping to extend friendship." But the iron hand would be displayed if the Mexicans fomented rebellion, Kearny roared.

Didn't that clash in a man's head? Wiley wondered; a promise first, then a threat. If he were a Mexican, he wouldn't react very well to something like that.

His eyes wandered to the formidable building across the plaza. Its very size made it impressive.

Wiley wanted to ask Elam what it was, but he didn't dare whisper. Something important, he imagined. Maybe it was some kind of a government building.

He would give anything to shift his buttocks. The discomfort started out as an itching, then slowly turned into actual hurting. He used all the swear words at his command at Kearny. But they had to be said under his breath, and it gave no help.

The ceremony finally ended, and the United States flag was run up its staff. The breeze had stiffened, and the flag crackled and snapped. It made Wiley kind of proud. Anybody could look at that flag and see that it was tough.

The troops were marched to the hill near the artillery and disbanded. The evening chores looked endless, and Wiley wanted to get them behind him so he could go into town. What if Buckley grabbed him and stuck him on some detail? The thought almost choked him.

He got his half shelter erected and ate his supper with Elam. It didn't seem possible, but Buckley hadn't spotted him yet.

"Did you get your pass, Daniel?"

Elam grinned. "Haven't you?"

"I'm afraid to ask Buckley. He might stick me for the whole night."

Elam laughed. "Company *C* drew all of the details tonight. We're all free."

"My God, why didn't you tell me?" Wiley started wolfing his food.

Ben Marshall wandered down the company street before they finished eating. He was a slight figure, the stamp of immaturity emphasizing the weak bone structure of his face. He claimed he was old enough to enlist, but Wiley thought he was a liar. He would put Marshall at no more than seventeen. He had watched Marshall scrape at the fuzz on his cheeks, but there wasn't enough beard to put a razor through a good workout. Marshall swaggered when he walked, and he was about as foulmouthed as any man Wiley had ever heard. He was a nuisance, and he had no close friends. He was passed from one man to the next in an attempt to get rid of him. Wiley didn't want him around, but he still felt a tinge of pity for him. Beneath the swagger and brag there was a loneliness. Marshall was the son of a Baptist preacher, and Wiley guessed he had been raised on too tight a rein. He had developed a streak of wildness to combat his father's dominion, and there was nothing too rash for him to prove that he was a man. Wiley was sorry for him but not sorry enough to want him hanging around.

Marshall peered into their mess tins. "You eating that slop again?" He described it with several choice oaths, and Elam gave him a pained look.

"Ben, you must work at trying to take a man's

appetite away." He got up, crossed the street, and dumped his mess tin in a garbage can.

If Marshall felt the affront, he didn't show it. "I'm going to eat something good tonight. I'm going to eat in town."

Elam felt a need to sting him. "How do you know it's good, Ben? Do you know what native cooking is like?" He described it without using obscenity, and a tinge of green stole across Marshall's face.

Wiley grinned. Elam was doing real well in getting even with Marshall.

Elam laughed at the woebegone look on Marshall's face. "I'm just funning you, Ben. I don't know what it's like. I've never eaten it."

Marshall's face brightened. "I knew you were just making it up. You two going into town tonight?"

Wiley wanted to say no and get rid of him. But Elam was too tenderhearted. "We're going in, Ben. You want to go in with us?"

Wiley smothered his need to swear. They wouldn't be able to get rid of Marshall now.

Marshall snickered. "I'm going in for the real same reason you two are."

Wiley glared at him. "What's that?"

Marshall could put more nastiness in a wink than any man Wiley ever saw. "Don't try to fool me, Wiley. I've heard Santa Fe is just full of women waiting for U.S. soldiers. Some say two bits will buy any of them. I'm liable to buy three or four before this night is through."

Wiley shook his head in disgust. Marshall was at his old trick of trying to let his mouth prove he was a man. His callowness stuck out all over him, and Wiley doubted he had ever been close to a woman.

He wanted to wipe that smirk off his face. "Ben, I'll bet you don't even know what a woman is for."

Marshall howled his outrage. "I'll show you. You just watch me."

He whipped around and stalked away from them.

Elam sighed. "You put the proof square up to him. Now we've got to keep an eye on him."

Wiley didn't intend to watch Marshall do whatever he had in mind. He wanted to find a woman too, but not the same kind Marshall talked about. He couldn't strike out on his own to find Linda, if he had to wet-nurse Ben Marshall.

Elam had argument in his face, and Wiley said stubbornly, "Why should I worry about him?"

"Because he can get into trouble. He's a pup, and it sticks out all over him. The first woman who picks him up can see it. When she gets through with him, he won't have the shirt left on his back."

"That's his lookout."

"Come on," Elam said patiently. "Let's keep him in sight."

Some of Wiley's temper faded as they entered Santa Fe. Night was kinder to it, and the torches softened its harsh outlines. He thought he would have only a sneering contempt for it, but it must be the crowded streets that excited him. He found himself as eager as a child, turning his head in every direction.

Elam was well-read on it, and he could talk almost as well versed as though he had been here.

"These are old houses," he said as they passed the first house on the outskirts. "I've read there's really gracious living in a house like this, but this outer wall is all we'll see of it."

Wiley stared at that wall. The house sat on the River Santa Fe, and the smell of honeysuckle drifted to him. He heard the faint strain of a guitar, then a burst of delighted feminine laughter. It aroused a loneliness in him, and he couldn't explain why it seized such a grip on him.

He looked quickly at Elam, feeling sure his expression had given him away. But Elam's eyes seemed remote and faraway. Wiley wondered if he had had the same feeling.

"Come on," Elam said gruffly. "We've lost sight of Ben."

Wiley spit into the street. "That's no loss. I hope we don't run into him again."

A woman stopped before them in the light of

a torch, and Wiley stared in amazement. She rolled a cigarette, and her fingers showed much practice. She poured tobacco out from a small tube onto a piece of cornhusk. She fashioned the cornhusk, stuck it into her mouth, and lit it. The brief flash of the match put her face into sharp display.

She wasn't attractive, let alone pretty. He saw the smallpox pits in her face, and her teeth were yellow. Her dress was ragged and soiled, and her bare feet were dirty. Her eyes were her only attractive feature, dark and shining. They flashed a bold message to Wiley and Elam. A man didn't have to know her language to understand it. That message was universal.

Her eyes changed at the lack of their response to her invitation. She shrugged in fatalistic acceptance, then her eyes turned murky under quick-springing rage. "Gringos," she hissed and spat into the sand.

Her hips had an insolent, swaying movement as she walked away. Wiley grinned. "She's had some practice at that, too. How did she get her teeth so yellow?"

"From the cornhusks. I suspect she's been smoking most of her life."

"How old is she?"

Elam looked thoughtful. "I'd say not over fifteen or sixteen." He saw Wiley's startled expression. "These women start pretty early. And they'll be old and look it before they're twenty-five."

Wiley grinned. "That's the kind Ben wants to find."

"I hope not. For both of their sakes." Elam fell into a thoughtful silence, and Wiley didn't try to break it.

Night, the smoking, hazy lights, and the throng of people gave an unreal glamour to the rutted, crowded streets. Several two-wheeled carretas passed them, and Wiley saw why they were built that way. They were the ideal vehicles to pass through the narrow streets. He also saw what had made the ruts in the streets. The cart wheels fitted them, and the ruts would remain unmelting until the next rain.

Indians, wrapped in bright-colored blankets, stalked their light-footed way through the crowds. Others sat, their backs against a building, their eyes inscrutable. The faces fascinated Wiley. They looked as though they were harshly hewn out of a dark, wooden block and showed no more expression than the block itself. Wiley wondered if they ever let a thought show on their faces.

In front of the long gallery, vendors sold an odd assortment of merchandise. If the eye couldn't identify it, the nostrils could. Soap, goat's cheese, onions, freckled beans were heaped in piles, some of them intermingling. A man could buy fire-wood, a few sticks, or a load more than enough to burden a burro. Fresh-cut alfalfa was twenty-five cents a load, and that was a good, familiar smell.

His nose wrinkled at the reek of rancid pork. Freshly killed and plucked chickens and bloody tripe were under pink cotton netting. The netting was a concession to the ever abundant flies. Even at night, the torchlight attracted them.

They wandered through the streets, intrigued by each new sight. San Francisco Street ran flush up against the base of the buildings, and the walls were blank and windowless. Elam said those were houses, and he imagined the poorer people lived in them. All along the sidewalks women were cooking chili and tamales on braziers. The fuel had a pungent, crisp smell, and Wiley didn't recognize it. Some kind of wood he had never seen burning before. It burnt quickly and left a white ash.

The hot, spicy aroma of the food carried to him, and he caught at Elam's arm. "Let's try some."

Elam's face was doubtful. "We don't know how it's made, or even what it is."

Wiley couldn't be turned. He was tired of the monotonous army food. He ordered by signs, and the woman put some chili on a cornhusk and placed a tamale beside it. Wiley took an incautious bite. His eyes watered, and his mouth burned. He gasped as he tried to fan fresh air into his mouth, and Elam enjoyed his fix.

"I tried to tell you. These people cook with peppers and hot spices. They're used to it."

"Try it." Wiley thrust the cornhusk at Elam.

Elam backed away. "I know how it is by just watching you."

"It's not that bad." It wasn't. It had a distinctive flavor. If it weren't so damned hot, Wiley thought he would like it. He tried another bite, much smaller than the first one. By rolling it around in his mouth before he swallowed it, he could handle it.

"I like it."

Elam's eyes twinkled. "I'll buy you another order."

Wiley grinned in wry admission. "This will do me for a while." But he wouldn't be surprised if he found himself trying chili and tamales again.

They wandered back toward the plaza, going through Burro Alley. It was crowded with wood choppers and their loaded, shaggy, diminutive animals. Wiley wondered how all of them made a living, and if the market was big enough to consume all that they cut. He wouldn't call it much wood; it fell more into the stick class. He looked at the wood choppers' ragged, worn clothing. They didn't appear to get much of a living out of their labor.

Some of the traders had moved their wagons to the plaza and were doing what looked to be a brisk business. Wiley and Elam stood around, watching the trading. The traders wore stained hickory jackets or blue fustian, and all of them smelled like wheel dope and mules. Plug tobacco was a favorite trading item. It was cased with licorice and molasses, and Wiley felt saliva start in his mouth. He had been out of chewing for a long time, and the smell of it brought back the memory of the taste of it.

The traders had a variety of goods; candlewick and cotton drill, shoes and cutlery. Wiley noticed how wistful the Mexicans' eyes were at the sight of the shoes, but very few pairs of them were sold. It wasn't hard to guess that the cost of the shoes was beyond their means. The Mexicans were fascinated by the display of assorted knives. They didn't buy very many of the knives either. Actually, they bought very little of anything. A lot of haggling went back and forth, and the traders had to work hard to sell an occasional item. The want shone in the people's eyes, but they didn't buy. It wasn't hard to see the reason; they simply didn't have the money.

Boredom caught up with Wiley's interest. "Daniel, I could take a drink."

"I won't argue against that, Wiley. I wonder how bad they'll rob us."

Wiley didn't have much money in his pocket. He shrugged. "I can tell you it won't be too bad. I can't last that long."

The La Fonda Inn was at the southwest corner

of the plaza, and was the biggest establishment of its kind in town. It had an enormous main barroom, and the gambling hall was off of it. Wiley had never seen anything like it. He contrasted it with the shabby little cardrooms in Weston, Missouri, and grimaced. Before every faro dealer was an ivory card box, inlaid with silver. The chuck-a-luck cage looked as though it was made of gold. Monte games were painted in bright colors on some kind of green material that covered the table. Every gaming table was made of walnut, its legs finished off in claws, and silver inlay had been worked into the carved edges.

Chips and money were stacked all over the tables, and Wiley stared about in awe. "By God, Daniel, did you ever see anything like this?"

Elam dumbly shook his head. "We don't belong in here."

Wiley knew what he meant. The sight of all that money made a man giddy. He started to turn, and Elam asked, "Where do you suppose all those doors go?"

The doors opened off one side, and Wiley compared it with the two or three doors leading off the cardroom in Weston. "I imagine for private games. The more money a man gets, the more privacy he wants. I guess these wealthy spies are no different."

Elam looked anxiously about the room. They were the only two soldiers in it, and it was crowded with Mexicans. Many of them wore expensive clothes. Velvet suits, of all colors, rubbed shoulders with green corduroy jackets, and black kid shoes were polished to a high luster.

One of the Mexicans stared at them, and Elam was sure there was malice in his eyes. The black velvet suit fitted his slight figure to perfection, and his hair was queued.

"Watch what you're calling them, Wiley. One of them is glaring at us. He must understand English; at least, enough to know what you called him."

Wiley turned his head to follow Elam's eyes. The man still stared at them. He felt the hostility in the man's eyes, and his own gorge rose. "Who cares?"

"I do," Elam answered. "He's not very big, and he doesn't look very dangerous. But his eyes are pure poison. And I think he could stick a knife into our ribs as well as a bigger man could."

Wiley grinned. "I won't worry you anymore. I'll watch what I say when they can hear. I've been called a gringo by them just a little while ago, and it didn't upset me."

Elam laughed. "That was from one of their women. A man can put more sting into it."

"I'll worry about it when it happens. Let's get that drink."

They crowded their way to the bar, and the bartender spoke enough broken English to make himself understood. Taos Lightning was twenty-five cents a drink. He had more difficulty in making the rest of it understood, and before he got it to them, both of his hands were gesturing.

Wiley chortled. Those hands had an eloquence of their own. "I'll be damned, Daniel. Army brass buttons are worth twenty-five cents apiece at this bar. He's even offering us a knife to cut them off with."

He reached for the knife, but Elam stopped him. "It's worth knowing, Wiley. But as long as we've got a little money, let's save the buttons. I've got a hunch if you turn up at some formation with some of your buttons missing, you'll do some walking for it."

Wiley nodded solemn agreement. He had had enough of his share of walking with sand-filled packs. Elam had a way of being right. The buttons could be saved until a dire emergency arose.

Elam grabbed his arm. "Look at who's down at the end of the bar."

Wiley craned his neck. "Well, I'll be god-damned. I wouldn't have believed it."

Ben Marshall stood at the far end of the bar, and he had two women with him. Neither of them had any appeal for Wiley. One was too fat, the other too thin, and both had the predatory face of a harpy. Didn't Marshall realize what had hold of him?

He downed the Taos Lightning in one gulp, and that was a mistake. His mouth felt as though he had thrust a bunch of lighted matches into it, and he couldn't breathe or swallow. His eyes ran water, and he couldn't have gotten a word out if he had to.

Elam watched him with no pity. "You always rush in, don't you? Did you expect a drink in here to be mellow and smooth?"

He took a sip of his glass and murmured, "I see what you mean."

Wiley's breathing returned to normal, and he ran his tongue around in his mouth. He was surprised to find it to be moving all right. "I'll take the next one easy," he promised.

Ben Marshall came by them, a woman on each arm. Wiley wasn't sure who was pulling whom out of here.

Marshall hooted at them; he was at the height of his glory. "I told you, didn't I? By God, I showed you." He had been at the liquor. His face was flushed, his eyes glassy.

Elam watched the three leave the building, and his eyes were speculative. "I think he's bitten off more than he can handle, Wiley. We'd better follow him. He may be heading for deep trouble."

"You heard his bragging. I don't give a good damn what happens to him."

"He may be found in some alley in the

morning. Didn't you take a close look at those two women?"

Wiley had. He remembered the viciousness; those had been two tough faces. "Maybe we'd better follow them," he said grudgingly.

They stopped outside and looked about them. For an instant, Wiley thought Marshall and the two women were out of sight, then he caught a glimpse of them turning into the mouth of an alley, almost a block down the street. It looked as though what Elam had predicted might happen was happening. Marshall was a goddamned fool. Didn't he have any better sense than to go into a place like that with those two?

"I was afraid of something like this," Elam said grimly.

They broke into a run and reached the alley just as a muffled voice yelled, "Hey, what are you doing? Let go of me." Fright put volume into the voice and made it ragged. "Help. Help."

The alley was dark, but movement picked out a spot ahead. Wiley saw a tumbling, heaving mass. He couldn't tell how many were involved, but it looked like more than the three that went into the alley.

A figure tried to run, and the rest of the mass overpowered and bore it to the ground. Marshall yelled again, "My God! She's got a knife. She's going to stab me!"

Four figures had Marshall smothered beneath

them. All of them were women, Wiley thought in amazement. Two others must have been waiting in the alley.

He was tempted to stand by and let it go on for a while longer, but he saw an arm rise and hover a moment over Marshall's chest. That might be a flash of light striking something in the hand. He bounded forward, snatched and caught the wrist, and his fingers bit deep into it. He twisted the wrist, and the fingers opened. He heard the clink of metal strike against the ground. The woman said something in a low, furious tone that he couldn't understand, and she tried to bite his hand. He jerked her from the pile and tossed her to one side.

"Watch them, Daniel," he warned. "That one had a knife."

He pulled another woman to her feet, and she turned a wild face toward him and tried to claw him. He ducked the swiping, hooked hand and cuffed her in the face. She staggered back several steps and fell.

Elam pulled the third one to her feet and shoved her away. Wiley jerked the last one erect and spun her. He planted a kick in her backsides and sent her stumbling down the alley.

Only one of them was left close to Marshall now, and that sounded like terror in her voice. Her voice rose higher and higher as she fled down the alley.

Wiley kneeled beside Marshall. Marshall babbled and sniffled. He had taken a mauling, but Wiley thought there was more fright in him than hurt.

"Ben, are you hurt?"

Marshall sat up, and his fingers clutched at Wiley's arm. "My God, I'm hurt. Did you see them? At least a dozen or more. They all had knives, and they cut me."

Wiley's finger's went over his torso. He couldn't feel any moist spots, and he couldn't see any darker patches that would mean bleeding.

"Stop that," he said in disgust. "Four women jumped you. And you're not cut. Goddam it, stop that sniffling and show me the bleeding."

Marshall felt all over himself. He had trouble getting his voice under control. "I thought I saw her use a knife. I tell you I felt it."

Wiley felt no sympathy. "You were so damned scared you imagined it."

Marshall fumbled through his pockets. He found something he wasn't imagining. "They robbed me. They took every cent I had."

Elam sounded as though he was filled with equal disgust. "You could've been dead. You're alive. It's worth what it cost you."

"I'll have them arrested," Marshall howled. "I'll have . . ."

"You'll do nothing," Wiley snapped. "You don't know them, and I doubt if you would if you saw them again. Do you want it to get all over camp that Ben Marshall got the hell beat out of him by four women?"

Marshall gaped at him.

"Think what the camp will do with this. They'll make your life plain hell."

"Wiley, you wouldn't tell them, would you?"

"The next time I catch you bragging about anything, I'll tell it. You're the one who decides that I tell it or not."

Marshall babbled his thanks until Wiley couldn't stand it any longer.

He hoisted Marshall to his feet. "Get on back to camp." He wanted to boot him, but he held that. Marshall scuttled down the alley. Those odd, choking sounds Elam was making was his effort to smother his laughter.

Wiley grinned sourly. "Do you think he learned anything?"

"I doubt it. He might stop bragging when we're near him. And he'll avoid us all he can. He'll have no love for us because we know what happened. You ready to go back?"

"Might as well." The morose mood was creeping in on Wiley again. Getting rid of Marshall would be worth something. But he had wasted an evening. He should have gone in alone and spent the evening looking for Linda and Dorsett.

NINE

Army camp life was a deadly, monotonous procession of the days. The only thing that made them bearable was passes into town, and Buckley had control of them. For four days he had turned Wiley down, and Wiley was going wild under it. He knew Buckley to be one tough, son-of-a-bitching sergeant. He didn't have to hold Wiley's pass to prove it.

Buckley didn't leave an unfilled minute in Wiley's day. In between the details were the drills twice a day. Wiley didn't curse Buckley, but surely Buckley could read it on his face. He had to face three roll calls a day, at daybreak, at sundown, and at tattoo. And he had better not be late for any of them, or Buckley would have him marching in front of the guard tent, two hours on and two hours off. The saddlebags were filled with forty pounds of sand, and at the end of two hours walking they doubled at least in weight.

Wiley glared at the yellow aspens on the high red slopes of the Mountain of the Blood of Christ. The sun was at just the angle to bring out that striking blending of color. He had looked at it before, caught by the display, but now nothing could soothe him. If Buckley turned him down on another pass, he was going to go straight to

Doniphan. If he kept his temper and stated it calmly, the colonel would listen to him. Doniphan wouldn't stand for rank pushing around a lower man beyond a reasonable level.

He found Buckley, and his face was hard. "Buckley, do I get my pass?"

Buckley grinned sardonically at him. "I thought you'd be after it." He pulled it out of his pocket already made out. He enjoyed seeing Wiley standing there openmouthed. "Let me tell you one thing, Anderson. Raise any kind of ruckus in town, and you'll never see another pass, if you're in the army for the rest of your life."

Wiley kept his wanted explosion in check. Buckley sounded as though Wiley Anderson and trouble traveled in the same harness. He avoided trouble whenever he could. A voice whispered in his ear, What about Dorsett?

He tucked the pass into his shirt pocket and turned away. Dorsett was a different matter, a special case. No man could point a finger at Wiley, regardless of what he did to him. What about Linda? He didn't know; he hadn't thought through that yet.

He ducked out of camp before supper, wanting to avoid Elam. Wiley had to be alone tonight. He had no clear idea of how to go about locating Dorsett. Hang around the traders' camp, he supposed, and hope he was lucky enough to pick up a scrap of information.

• • •

Rocha spread his hands apologetically. "Señor, as I have told you, I could not reach Señor Hendricks. I tried, but the soldier stopped me. I swallowed the paper as you told me. The soldiers wanted to know what I was doing out there, but I talked to none of them."

"You've told me a dozen times before," Dorsett said wearily. If Rocha thought he had earned the second half of the payment, he was crazy. He hadn't delivered the message.

His face set in gloomy lines. He couldn't blame Rocha for the miscarriage of his plans. Even if Rocha had reached Hendricks, it would have done no good. His market had disappeared.

He pulled a cigar from his breast pocket and savagely bit off its end. That bastard Armijo, running the way he did. He had heard that American money filled Armijo's pockets, and he didn't doubt it; that plus what Armijo had been able to loot from the treasury should have really filled his pockets.

He cursed Armijo for treachery until he ran out of oaths. Wasn't he involved in the same kind of business? Armijo had only beaten him to the punch. He smiled wanly at his self-accusation. What was he going to do with those rifles? Every time he saw Hendricks, the man threw the question at him. Hendricks was uncomfortable with those rifles under the floor boards of the wagons, and his money was in them too. Dorsett didn't blame him for his anxiety. The same thing was driving him wild. But he couldn't do anything with those rifles until he found a customer to deliver them to, and it had to be a wealthy one.

That was the problem that was grinding him into the ground. He would bet there were a hundred important men in Santa Fe who would have given anything for those rifles; anything but what they didn't have—money. Dorsett had delicately probed the subject with Yocupico, and he had seen the fire light in those black eyes. But when Dorsett had mentioned money, Yocupico had raised and lowered his hands in helpless despair.

"But do not leave Santa Fe, Señor," he had begged. "I have many friends, patriots who are ready to fight for New Mexico's defense." His eyes had a fanatical gleam. "With those rifles we can run the gringos back where they came from." The gleam faded. "But they are like I am. Armijo stripped our pesos, and the hard times he created make it even worse. Give me time. I will talk to my friends. It is a great sum, but perhaps together we can raise it. But it will have to be slow. I cannot openly talk to them. The Americanos are already here." It looked as though a shiver ran through him. "They must not hear anything about it, or their wrath will descend on us. Let me have the rifles before they know anything about it, and we will send them fleeing."

It was hard for Dorsett to keep his cynical smile hidden. He doubted that, but he didn't give a damn which side won. All he wanted was to deliver the rifles and get his money out of them.

"I'll hang around a little longer," he had told Yocupico. "Then I'll take my wagons farther south. Maybe as far as Chihuahua City. Surely there are Mexicans who place their patriotism above their pesos?"

That had put a darkening into Yocupico's face; that had stung him deep.

Dorsett looked at his companion. "Rufino, you didn't get in touch with Yocupico today?"

Rocha looked as though he wanted to cry. He had learned to his sorrow that he didn't get paid for unfulfilled missions.

"Señor, I went to his house five times today. I waited outside the wall until my feet ached. You said I could talk to nobody but him. Then who was I to talk to?" His face was eloquent with unhappiness. "I did not see him come out or go in."

Dorsett nodded. Yocupico was probably occupied talking to his friends. As he said, it would be a slow, furtive business, and it could not be hurried.

"Try to see him again tomorrow."

He stopped short and caught Rocha's arm. A

blue uniform and cap were on the corner ahead of them. How he hated the sight of them, and Santa Fe was filled with them. Every time he caught sight of one of those uniforms, his heart jumped and swelled. He had questioned Hendricks about Wiley Anderson, and Hendricks had said, "I saw him outside of Leavenworth. I remembered him from seeing him in Liberty. He was asking questions about you." Hendricks had rubbed his jaw reflectively. "He packs a wallop. And he wants to find you real bad."

That had put an almost overwhelming despair in Dorsett. Every time he stepped outside, he had been afraid he would step into Anderson. Anderson would try to kill him on sight. He was sure of that. He couldn't get down off this pair of horns he was riding. If he killed Anderson, the army would prosecute him. If they found out his real background, then nothing he could say would save him. The thought-filled hours of the nights were driving him crazy.

Rocha stared at the blue uniform. The man's back was turned toward them, but Rocha looked as though he might know him.

Dorsett's fingers bit deeper. "Do you know him? Who is it?"

"I cannot be sure, Señor. He is tall like the one who put the rifle barrel into my back, and he stands no straighter. It could be the same one."

Dorsett felt the panic building in him. He had

questioned Rocha thoroughly about the man who had arrested him, but Rocha hadn't known. But then how could he know? He had never seen Wiley Anderson before. Wouldn't it be a hellish turn of luck, if Dorsett ran into Wiley now?

"Do you want me to say something to him, Señor?"

"No, goddam it—" Dorsett tensed and broke off. The blue uniform was turning. The man stood beside a torch, and its smoky illumination was enough to put his face into a good enough light.

Dorsett gasped. Fear was a hard stone in his chest. It wasn't imagination that was feeding his terror. That was Wiley Anderson.

Anderson was looking around; he had seen nothing as yet that fixed his attention.

"Rufino, listen carefully. That man will probably try to arrest you again. We will go back to the corner before we separate. It will give you a better chance to get away from him. If he sees me with you, he will yell for me to hold you. And I have to obey him. If he discovers us, run hard. Do you understand me?"

Rocha's eyes were big. He would do exactly as Señor Dorsett said. He did not want the Americano to arrest him again.

Dorsett forced himself to keep a casual pace. Had Anderson turned completely around? Was he showing any interest in them? He dreaded the thought of a shout directed at them. He could breathe a little easier; they were almost at the corner, and the shout hadn't come.

"You! Stay where you are."

Dorsett groaned as the strident notes of the shout went through him. That wasn't yet recognition in Anderson's voice, but it could be the beginning of it. He wanted to get near enough to take a clear look at him.

"Run," he breathed to Rocha and whipped around the corner.

Maybe it was Rocha in whom Anderson was interested. Dorsett hoped so, but he didn't have much to bolster it. The yell came again, this time louder and more positive. The hope was dead; Anderson was after him. His running was a dead giveaway, riveting Anderson's attention on him. But what else could he do? He couldn't stand and wait for Anderson to walk up to him.

He was almost to the end of the next block when he heard the slam of footsteps. He looked back, and Anderson was pounding along behind him. In a prolonged foot race, Dorsett was sure Anderson would run him down; the man was younger and in better physical shape. Running by itself wasn't going to be enough.

He turned to his left at the next corner, and almost ran down a woman coming toward him. He did a fast side step and managed to just brush her. His lungs were beginning to heat and labor. He ducked into the nearest alley and ran down it. He had one advantage, though he didn't know how much strength it had. He knew Santa Fe, every street, every alley, every foot lane. If he could only build up enough of a lead on Anderson, he could lose him in one of these devious alleys.

He looked back as he cleared the alley, and he clutched at a vain hope that he had lost him. But there he came, bursting out of the alley. He looked back again and saw Anderson glance around, trying to pick him up again. He had gained a few steps, but he didn't dare stop running. The movement picked him out for Anderson. If he could only increase the lead until he could turn a corner, or duck into some place where he wouldn't be seen.

He remembered the *cantina* on the next street over; it had a rare thing, a back door. If he could get to its entrance without being seen, he could run through it, come out of the rear doors, and slip away through the back yards that formed a trackless maze.

He put on his last burst of speed, forcing cruel demands upon his legs. He turned the corner and angled across the street to the *cantina*'s door. He reached it, stepped inside, and dared stop to ease his laboring lungs.

This was a poor place with a few sorry pieces of furniture scattered over the earthen floor. The few candles gave poor light. Five men sat at one of the tables, and they watched him with veiled hostility. Ordinarily, he wouldn't have picked this as the safest of places for a lone American to wander into.

He peered out into the street, and Anderson wasn't yet in sight. Maybe he had lost him. The swelling elation was dashed. Anderson turned the corner and came down the street at a much slower pace, for he no longer had his quarry in view.

Dorsett did some quick thinking. He might slip through the back door and trust that Anderson never learned that he had entered the *cantina*. But it would be better to strengthen his chance. Anderson might see some passer-by who could have seen Dorsett run into here, and he would be on the hunt again.

Dorsett looked at the five men, and at the one standing behind the shabby bar. The faint candlelight picked up an animal-like gleam in their eyes. The six of them were as rough-looking characters as Dorsett had ever seen. It wouldn't take many centavos to buy them, and if they cut Anderson's throat, he wouldn't be sorry.

His eyes burned as the idea developed. He could cover his back track, and if Anderson came in here, the trail would abruptly end. He had enough pesos in his pocket to more than buy these six men.

He strode to the table, and they watched every move. No eye would hold on him. Each time he tried to fix one, it would slide away.

He pulled out a thick wad of the greasy, soiled native money and threw it onto the table.

"Your money," he said in fluid Spanish. "A very bad man follows me, a man dressed like an American soldier. But he is not. He is only a thief and murderer. Keep him from following me and don't tell him which way I went." He waved his hand at the money. "The money is yours. Divide it up between you."

Those eyes were black marbles, but there was a changing in them, a change toward him. The eyes had a glistening shine as they glanced from the money to him. They could pocket the money once he was gone, and betray him, but he thought he had bought them.

He frowned as he warned them, "Do not tell this bad man that you have money. He will take it from you."

The fattest, swarthiest one had a nasty chuckle. "Señor, he may try. No more."

Other chuckles joined him. "*Vaya*, Señor. He will stop here."

Dorsett hurried toward the back door. He looked back and all of the men had turned to face the door. Dorsett had an impulse to laugh wildly. It was too bad he wasn't going to be here to see Anderson get the welcome arranged for him.

• • •

Wiley swore as he stood on the corner. This was the wildest goose chase he had ever been on. He had questioned thirty people, and most of them had given him blank looks in return. He had hung around the traders' camp, and he hadn't come up with a thing. How many faces had he looked into tonight? How many people had he overtaken to have the disappointment return as he saw that the face wasn't the one he wanted? His weariness was pulling at him and dulling his thoughts. He knew one thing; he had to have a better plan for locating Dorsett, or he could spend a million nights in the same futile hunt. Why, Dorsett could be on the next street over, and Wiley wouldn't know it.

He glanced around, not having any real belief that he would see Dorsett, but in the sheer desperation of needing something to do. He saw two men down at the darker end of the block. He thought the smaller one Mexican by his lack of height and the big hat he wore. The bigger one towered over him, and excitement began to tick in his pulses. He remembered Dorsett as a tall man, preferring a white hat, and this man wore one.

His interest kept sharpening. Those two had stopped; were they talking about him? He knew what his imagination was doing to him. He wanted to see Dorsett so badly that his imagination created a mocking brush that painted every face he wanted to see. Could he have been lucky enough to stumble on Dorsett?

The pair turned, and Wiley thought their stride showed new purpose.

"You," he bawled. "Stay where you are."

The yell prodded them into a run, and he tore after them. They split on him at the corner, and he didn't give a damn about the Mexican. His surety that the other was Dorsett had increased, or why was he in such wild flight?

He lost ground in an alley, picked it up on a straightaway, and lost some more at a corner. At every corner he had to stop and look around to see which direction the man had taken, and that lost him a few steps. But the conviction had grown within him; he was going to run him down.

He turned into a new street, and this was in a poorer, darker part of town. The running figure wasn't in sight, and Wiley knew an overwhelming wash of disappointment. Which direction had the man taken this time? The one he picked could easily be wrong.

A bent figure came down the street toward him, and Wiley stepped in front of him. He saw alarm fill the old, wrinkled face.

"Did you see a man run down this street?" he demanded.

"Quien sabe?"

Wiley knew a sickness; he had chased Dorsett this far, and now he had lost him, unless he made this Mexican understand.

He didn't know any Spanish, and he couldn't recall the few words he had heard. He ran in place, simulating a man in flight. "*Americano*," he said several times. He pointed at some of the buildings. Elam could speak Spanish. He had tried to teach Wiley a few phrases, and Wiley wished he had listened to him. Was *que* the Spanish for which? He pointed at the line of buildings and said, "*Que*, *que*?"

The old man's face brightened. He pointed at a building up the street. "*Americano*? *Si*, *si*."

Wiley pressed his shoulder before he broke into a run again. He only prayed that the Mexican had understood him.

This was a poorly lighted building, and time and weather had badly beaten it. He hesitated a moment before he stepped inside. He didn't have the slightest idea of what he was walking into, but if Dorsett had gone into here, Wiley wouldn't find him by standing out on the street.

Five men were seated around a table, but they had turned their chairs to face the door. The bartender was at the end of the bar, and there was an odd alertness in him too.

Dorsett wasn't in the room, and the disappointing sickness filled Wiley again. He had never gotten a good look at Dorsett, but he had been so sure that was him. Before he said a word about Dorsett, he knew he was going to have trouble with the language again.

"*Americano*. Did he run in here?" Wiley measured with his hand to the top of his head. "*Americano. Muy grande*." He didn't remember whether *grande* meant tall or fine.

Several heads shook back and forth. They watched him with wary eyes, and they reminded Wiley of the way a crouching cat watched a hovering bird. Why did they have this much interest in him? Had Dorsett known them and ordered them to stop him here?

It could be. His muscles ached with the new rigidity stealing into them. If they were here to stop him, he would probably find out quickly enough.

"I think he ran through here. Don't you have a back door? I'll just go out there and look around."

Some of them knew enough English to understand him. He heard the rapid exchange of staccato words, then the bartender stepped out before him.

He violently shook his head. "No, Señor. *Vaya*."

Wiley tensed. He had passed the table, and five men were behind him. His move toward the bar had brought out some kind of menace. Another step or two would define it.

"Pardon me." He reached out a hand to push the bartender aside.

That was the fuse that exploded everything. The bartender shoved both of his hands into Wiley's chest and knocked him backward. He staggered until he caught his balance, and the five behind him were on him. They got in each other's way, and most of the blows were misdirected, but they bore Wiley down by sheer weight.

He heaved at them, knowing he had to get to his feet again or they would beat the life out of him. The reek of bad wine filled his nostrils. He found no great power in any of them; it was just the numbers that were overwhelming him.

He made a violent roll, taking two with him, and leaving the others. He rose to his feet, carrying both of them with him, and he shook them off him, like a terrier does after emerging from the water.

He sent one spinning away and sloughed the other in the belly, exploding a great puff of gagging hurt. He had a vital split second, and he took it, using his speed and agility to get something solid and protective at his back.

He picked up a chair as he ran toward the wall. He put his back against it and raised the chair, holding it by its back. He bared his teeth. "Come on, you bastards." He wasn't frightened, just thoroughly angry.

One of them rolled on the floor, holding his sick belly. His groans had enough volume to reach the street. The others approached cautiously, the bartender joining them. He had broken off the base of a bottle, and he held the jagged neck. Wiley was surprised the others hadn't yet drawn knives. He had to count on his speed and the rickety chair he held, making each swing accurate and vicious. When he got a lick at a man, he had better put him down for good, for he might not get the second chance.

The fan of men slowly moved toward him, and their caution said they had respect for him. Not enough, Wiley thought with grim humor; they still came at him.

He picked out the two in the middle, judging he might get through the smallest. He bounded forward, the chair swinging in a great arc off his shoulder. Its legs caught one man in the face and broke against the side of another's head. He held a leg of the chair, and the rest of it was little better than matchstick timber. He dashed through the broken line before it could solidly react. A hand did grab his sleeve, and he felt the material give at his shoulder.

The sheer speed left them blinking, and it adjusted the odds a little but still not enough in his favor. He couldn't get to the front door; they were between it and him, and he wasn't sure where the back door was.

He ran across the room to get another wall at his back and on the way discarded the chair leg. He wanted something heftier. He picked up a six-foot, crudely made wooden bench. It would be awkward to swing, but it had more weight, and if he could get enough muscle behind it, it should cut a swath.

He had three of them on the floor, the first one he had put there with a blow and the last two the chair had downed. One of these was stretched out unconscious, the others sat dully looking at the blood that splashed into their lap from their ruined faces.

The three left on their feet yelled ferocious curses at him; he knew they were furious by the sound of the words. He heard a few yells coming from the door. This had gone on long enough and was loud enough to draw a crowd. That crowd worried him. They would be natives, and they might join the ones in here.

The three shuffled toward him and two of them had drawn knives, the bartender still holding the broken bottle. The sight of the knives chilled his blood. He had always hated a naked blade. The thing he feared most was a thrown one; could he get the bench up in time to deflect it?

He saw a hand raise, and he threw up the bench, holding it shoulder and throat high. The blade thunked into it with considerable force, and a blade tip split the seat plank.

It put Wiley into an agony of apprehension. He could do only one thing, and he ran forward, holding the bench before him. His fear lent him speed and force, and he crashed the bench into the three of them. They went down, and he tried to leap over them. Clutching hands entangled his feet, and he tripped and fell. He threw the bench as far as he could from him, not wanting to fall on it.

Something fiercely hot traced a thin line on his thigh, and he opened his mouth and howled with the hurt. He pummeled with his fists and lashed out with his feet, and he clawed and kicked his way free of them.

He got up before any of them could, and he gasped for breath to ease the fire in his lungs. He aimed a kick at a head and connected with the bartender's. He had another knifeman to cope with, and it put a rising panic inside him. His head was filled with ringing noises, and he didn't know whether they came from within his head, or if the crowd outside had grown.

The other three were scrambling to their feet, and he grabbed a table and spun it toward them. He grabbed a chair and reached them before they cleared the table away. He was vaguely aware of a rending crash as the table slowly buckled on its legs and collapsed.

The hollering was worse outside the door, and he thought, They're coming in. He panted for each breath, and his leg stung and burned. Along the way he had picked up assorted bumps and bruises that he hadn't even been aware of until this moment. If those people outside came in, he didn't know what he was going to do with them. He still had two left of the original number that he hadn't handled yet.

A voice with more lung power than he had yet heard bellowed, "What the hell's going on in here?"

Wiley had never thought he would see the time when he was grateful to see Sergeant Buckley. He was now; he wanted to throw his arms around his neck.

Three American soldiers were behind Buckley, and Wiley felt like hugging them too.

Buckley's mouth sagged. "Not you again. By God, I warned you."

Wiley had to lean against a wall to keep from slumping slowly to the floor.

"Just a little disagreement, Sergeant."

Buckley looked around the room, and his eyes bugged. "Just you against them? You did all this to them and this room?" He shook his head in total disbelief, and for a moment he didn't know what to say or do.

He was beginning to think of something; his face was starting to turn redder. "This will go all the way up to Kearny. He's not very happy with just plain fraternization with the natives. That's enough to upset him. But you have to go all the way. You have to fight them."

Maybe it was funny, but Wiley didn't have

any funny reactions left in him. He was scared to death Buckley would bypass Doniphan and go straight to Kearny.

He shifted his weight on the aching leg. He could feel the moisture of his bleeding seep through his pants leg. "Doniphan won't be too happy about you going over his head."

Buckley saw the ripped material and the shining wetness around it. His voice changed. "Hell, you're cut. We've got to have something done for that."

It was the first time Wiley even felt like a weak grin. He couldn't imagine Buckley being concerned about him over anything.

TEN

Wiley had never seen Doniphan this angry before. The colonel paced back and forth before the small table in his tent, and he didn't say a word. Wiley thought he was too mad to risk speaking. He almost wished Doniphan would swear at him.

It may have been only a few minutes, but it seemed like an eternity before Doniphan faced and stabbed him with those piercing eyes. Buckley was smart; he had taken Wiley to Doniphan, stated what had happened, then skipped out of the tent.

"Wiley, you've heard General Kearny's orders?"

"Yes, sir." Wiley stood rigidly stiff. He was surprised by a kindness Buckley had done for him. Before taking him to Doniphan, Buckley had had the leg bandaged. It wasn't a deep cut, and it had stopped bleeding, but it still hurt.

"You know he's trying to keep the relations between the natives and the army on the highest level possible?"

"Yes, sir."

Doniphan groaned in despair. "But that didn't make any difference to you. You wrecked a *cantina*; you assaulted six Mexicans."

Wiley squirmed under those eyes. Damned if

they didn't make a man feel like he didn't have any place to hide.

"Why, Wiley?"

"They jumped me first, Colonel."

Doniphan shook his head in exasperation. "Why did you go in there? It's not the kind of a place an American would frequent."

"I guess I just wandered in, sir."

Doniphan tossed his hands. "It was that personal business of yours, wasn't it, Wiley?"

Wiley didn't dare admit to it. Doniphan had called it right when he said "personal business," and Wiley intended keeping it that way. He knew an inward sickness, not from the mauling, though he was well aware of it, but from being so close to Dorsett and not being able to lay his hands on him. His hands were tight fists. Another meeting would come with Dorsett; he would find him.

"How bad is that leg?" Doniphan asked abruptly.

"Not too bad, sir."

"Can you walk on it?"

Wiley inwardly groaned. That meant more walking hours. "I can walk."

Doniphan allowed a frosty smile to touch his lips. "I'm not giving you walking. That's not enough." Exasperation crossed his face again. "Don't you see what you could have done? There's too much unrest in Santa Fe as it is. You could have set it off. It was just lucky that Buckley and those other three happened by that door. That crowd attracted him, and he checked on it. What do you think he found? Wiley Anderson in another fight."

Wiley couldn't keep the grin off his face. "I guess he did."

"Stop that grinning," Doniphan roared. "I'll give you two days off before you report to the building of Fort Marcy. Maybe that'll wear some of the spoiling out of you."

That didn't sound too bad to Wiley. Kearny had ordered the building of the new fort and named it after the Secretary of War. The troops had made many ribald remarks about Kearny naming the fort after the secretary. Quite a few of the soldiers had volunteered for it. The rest of the roll would be filled out with military prisoners. They were supposed to be paid eighteen cents a day, though that didn't seem much consideration to Wiley. He hadn't heard of anybody getting their regular pay yet.

That didn't sound too bad, and Wiley couldn't help but sigh.

Doniphan caught it, and his eyes blazed. "You think that's all of it. You won't leave camp, day or night. That holds until I see some reason to change it. Buckley will keep a close eye on you. You sneak out, and I'll put all of the First Missourian out looking for you. Don't be fool enough to make another mistake."

Wiley saluted him smartly. He thought this

was one occasion that demanded it. "Yes, sir." His limping hardly showed as he left the tent.

Working on the fort wasn't so bad, though doing the same thing over and over was monotonous. Wiley learned a lot about making adobe bricks. Mexican laborers dug a hole in the ground, carried buckets of water to it, then mixed mud and straw. The soft mixture was poured into wooden forms, and after the sun had hardened them, the forms were lifted off the bricks. They weighed forty pounds, and while forty pounds wasn't heavy, it was the accumulation of the day that bore a man down. Wiley didn't learn to like adobe bricks, but he had a healthy respect for them. The outline of the fort began to take shape. Wiley groaned. It was going to take a hell of a lot of bricks to build it, and Doniphan probably wouldn't let him off until it was done.

The Mexican laborers had the right idea about work; lie down as close as you can to it and go to sleep. The sergeants spent a good portion of the day kicking them back onto their feet. Wiley wondered if the laborers were getting their pay. If they weren't, he didn't hear any complaints about it. At least they were being fed, and to a poor man that was a lot. This time, Wiley picked up as many Spanish phrases as he could learn. He learned that Armijo was *un tirano*, a tyrant, who robbed the poor through his increasing taxes. The poor were glad to see him gone.

"Does everybody feel that way?" Wiley asked a peon. It was amazing how much of a conversation two people could carry on, though the other's tongue was alien.

The peon spread out his hands. He could talk as eloquently with them as he could with his tongue. "Not all of the rich feel that way," he said darkly. "He made them rich. If they cannot have Armijo, they want another of the same kind."

Doniphan came back after Wiley had worked ten days in the mud hole. The mud had splashed onto his clothes and skin and hardened like iron. It took hard soaking to get it off of either.

He watched Wiley for a moment, frowning at him. Wiley thought in instant alarm, What have I done now? I haven't even been out of camp.

"Do you want a pass tonight?" Doniphan asked abruptly.

Wiley's eyes shone. Getting out of this camp would be like taking a short visit to heaven.

"Thank you, Aleck," he said softly.

Doniphan's frown deepened. "General Kearny's giving a big ball at the Governor's Palace tonight, for the illustrious Mexican families. He hopes it will smooth out relations between them and us."

Wiley's eyes sparkled. "You're not inviting me to the ball, are you, Aleck?"

The audacity of the question pulled a burst of laughter from Doniphan. "I can imagine the general appreciating that. But you do need a new uniform. You've about got all the miles out of that one. See if you can get a better one out of the supply wagon."

Wiley was grateful for that. A man hated going around looking like a scarecrow.

Doniphan's eyes drilled into him. "Wiley, no more trouble."

"No, sir." Wiley couldn't meet his eyes. It wouldn't do any good to promise that. He couldn't stop looking for Dorsett.

Wiley was lucky. The uniform came close to fitting. He thought he didn't look so bad tonight. Santa Fe's streets were packed. Every soldier in the army seemed to have his freedom tonight. On some of the streets Wiley couldn't go the way he wanted to; he could only drift with the direction of the crowd.

It was hopeless trying to pick a single face out of this mob. He doubted that Dorsett would be on the streets. But he might have enough standing to get an invitation to Kearny's ball. If so, he might attend that. Wiley could stand outside and watch the arrivals. It would be more likely that he would see Hendricks, and he frowned. It hadn't done him any good before.

He knew what he was going to do, but first,

he needed something to eat. His stomach could stand hot chili and tamales again.

The market stalls were underneath the palace's western tower, and soldiers and traders were packed before every one. A man had to wait patiently before he could get a place in front of one.

He listened absently to the soldiers and traders talk back and forth. It struck him with new awareness how raucous the Americans' talk was. The Mexicans' talk seemed like a whisper in comparison. Wiley made a wry face. He was sorry, but he would have to say the Americans were bigmouthed.

Lighted torches were set up on poles around the plaza, and their smoky, yellow light cast wavery, uncertain shadows. Red-skirted women sold cheese, soap, and tamales. He made certain he was before the stall he wanted and edged up another step as the line moved. He saw fresh cuts of buffalo hump and pork. It looked good, and he wished the woman was cooking that.

He paid for his tamales, and even wrapped in cornhusks they were hot. He shifted them from hand to hand and sauntered back to the plaza. The traders had built a bonfire near the sundial, and the sound of their laughter put a nostalgia in Wiley. He wished he had come in with Elam. But it wouldn't do to drag him into trouble not of his making.

He finished a tour of the plaza; the palace's front wall ran the entire length of the quadrangle. An open coach gate was at the end of the building, and a dragoon sentry was on duty.

Wiley felt no sympathy for him. No volunteer had any love for a regular. "It looks like they finally found a job you could handle," he jeered.

The dragoon glared at him. "Don't stand around here blocking the entrance, or I'll call the officer of the guard."

Wiley moved away. The dragoon would do just that, and the officer would be glad to arrest him. He had no doubt that both of them were probably unhappy about getting stuck with duty tonight.

He stopped a hundred feet away. That ought to be far enough away to satisfy the dragoon. A lighted torch pole was on each side of the gate; he could see anybody who went through it.

People started filing in. The Mexicans arrived in dusty coaches and dearborns, and Wiley was awed by their finery. The women were dressed in velvet and silks and displayed more bosom than Wiley had ever seen before out in public.

He paid close attention when the traders started arriving. Liquor showed in their loud bantering of each other. These were the owners and bosses of the wagons, for they wore dress hats and fancy fustian coats. They came in pretty much of a bunch, and Dorsett wasn't among them. He hadn't really expected to see him, but he had expected Hendricks to be here.

He noticed how the Mexicans and traders stayed apart and wondered if Kearny's ball would be a failure. A cynical thought hit him; a little food and a little music wasn't enough to make people like each other.

He jeered at the officers as they arrived; weren't they fancy now? They were dressed in plumed dress helmets, saber harness, jack boots, orange silk sashes, and yellow-striped britches.

Kearny came in shortly after, and he put his officers to shame. He wore a double-breasted dress coat with rows of gold bullion and bullion epaulettes. His dress hat had white horsehair plume. He was a hard-jawed man with gray hair brushed forward on brows and temples. This was one of the few times Wiley had seen him smiling. He guessed he was a good enough officer, but he would take Doniphan over him.

He enjoyed the display of finery. It was as though both races vied with each other, each trying to show the best. Wiley guessed he would have to hand it to the Mexicans.

The civilians wore black velvet coats and gold braid. The women wore the finest silks with mantillas lifted from their hair by mother-of-pearl combs. Wiley wondered what some of these dresses cost: enough, he would bet, to feed a poor family with kids for a year.

The Mexican officers really knocked his eyes out. They wore patent leather shakos with red pompons and black horsehair plumes. Their coats were finished off with brass buckles, gold aiguillettes, and scarlet saber sashes. The artillery officers were in red coats with green turnbacks. He would give them one thing; the Mexicans were sure as hell big on dress.

He moved a few feet to a building and leaned against it. He wondered if Elam was watching this from some place. He hoped he was. Elam would enjoy it.

ELEVEN

Maria's eyes snapped rebelliously at her brother. "You do not tell me we are not going until I am dressed for the ball. What am I supposed to do now?"

"Stay home," Perea Yocupico said unfeelingly. "I only came in to tell you that I cannot go to the ball."

He had just returned from seeing Dorsett, and Dorsett had demanded that he be helped out of Santa Fe tonight. The man was in a growing sweat of nerves. Perea had asked why he didn't go and take the wagons with him. Dorsett's swearing response wasn't directed at him, and that was good. The army would not permit the wagons to leave. Dorsett claimed his money was almost gone.

"I will help you leave tonight," Yocupico had told him. Dorsett used the threat of the hidden rifles like a whip. Yocupico had spent much time thinking about where those rifles could be, and ended up with nothing. He had even passed close to Dorsett's wagons and put a casual glance into the bed. He saw nothing that looked like boxes of rifles. He should have known Dorsett would not have brought the rifles into Santa Fe.

He clenched his teeth as he paced the room. He

had been pledged a little money but not nearly enough to purchase the rifles. These troubled times did not lend themselves to raising money. How well he knew that! He had sold part of his flock of sheep at ruinous prices. He would finance Dorsett's trip to Chihuahua City but no more.

"Where do you go out now?" Maria asked.

"Business," he said curtly.

Anger flushed her cheeks. "I know why we are not going. You do not want to mix with the Americanos. Couldn't the mixing be a good thing? Now that the fighting is over, couldn't we begin to accept them?"

His eyes were icy with repressed fury. "Never will I accept them." He had accepted the invitation to go to the ball because many of the big families had told him they were going. He could skillfully work on their nerves; he would point out the Americano arrogance, the insults they threw into a man's face. Yes, he could have done good work at that ball, but he couldn't now. He had to get Dorsett out of town.

He paused at the door. "I do not know how long I will be gone."

Maria raged at the closed door. Did Perea expect to make a prison out of this house? She had practically been chained to it ever since the Americanos came here. She hated them, she hated what they did to her people. She crossed herself and raised her eyes. Hating was a bad thing, but at times one could not help it.

Why would it be so wrong for her to go to the ball, even if Perea wasn't along to accompany her? All of the finest Mexican families would be there; they would keep an eye on her.

She picked up her mantilla and draped it carefully over the combs in her hair. She pulled it together before her and her head was lifted in defiance as she went out of the door. Perea would not like this, but she did not care. A house could drive a woman to screaming if she was confined to it too long.

She was frightened at the number of soldiers on the streets. She should have expected that. But if she hurried and minded her own business, they would pay her no attention.

She heard a few remarks tossed at her, and her English was good enough to understand the words. Her cheeks fired at the words. What she had been told was true. The Americanos were unmannered savages.

Her resolution was weakening by the time she reached the palace. She saw no Mexicans going into it, and she hesitated. The sentry seemed to have a leering look on his face, and she feared he might say something to her. She went several yards past the entrance before she turned. She would enter with the next Mexican family that arrived.

She waited a moment, and she couldn't help her growing dismay. Had she arrived too late? Perhaps no other Mexican families would come. She could not stand here. Other soldiers were wandering about the plaza, and her lack of motion would be an open invitation to them.

She passed the entrance again and did not pause as she had done before. She could not keep walking back and forth before the entrance. Once more, she told herself. Maybe one of the Mexicans will come to the doorway for some reason.

She was deluding herself, she thought. This was a mistake, she saw it clearly now. But she had been so disappointed and angry at Perea for ruining the evening that she had not thought clearly. Her best place was home, and she should get there as fast as she could go.

She pulled the mantilla over her face as two more soldiers passed her. Their following laughter were claws that scraped at her skin.

Wiley watched the Mexican girl walk back and forth before the door. By the richness of her dress he would say she belonged with the others inside. It was odd that she didn't step into the building. She wanted to, he was certain of that, but something was troubling her. Every time she passed through the torchlight, it picked out her profile, and he had been struck by the dusky cameo-like carving of her beauty. She was very young, he thought. But she was a woman, and she moved with a woman's grace.

He scowled as he thought the last pair of soldiers was going to accost her. Couldn't the damned fools see that she wasn't the kind of a woman who frequented the streets?

She must have made a quick decision, for she turned suddenly and walked away from the palace. It was more than curiosity about her, it was a worry that rode him hard. She should not be walking about these streets at night.

He followed her, keeping a good block behind her. Where the shadows were the thickest, he lost sight of her for a few steps. He wanted nothing more than to see her safely home. Some of the troopers would hoot at him, but he didn't have to explain anything to anybody.

She turned into a better section of town, and her danger had lessened to that degree. The troopers didn't hunt for company in this part of town.

A bulky shadow stepped out from apparently nowhere and blocked her way. Wiley was close enough to her to think he heard her gasp.

The two shadows merged, and she said indignantly, "Let go of me."

Wiley broke into a run. He didn't know who the bulky shadow was, but it made no difference. The figure meant her nothing but harm.

The two figures broke a little apart, and a male

voice said in hoarse anger, "Why, you little bitch. You clawed me." He sprang forward and caught her, and the struggle was more violent.

Wiley heard a cry slapped out of her. He thought the male voice was familiar, but he wasn't sure until he grabbed the shoulder and spun the man around.

He had worn a uniform coat long enough to know the feel of its material. And even in this darkness, the enraged face was thoroughly familiar.

Shannon, he thought. The sour reek of liquor fanned his face. Shannon was ugly enough sober; liquor only fired him up that much quicker.

Wiley wasn't a match for Shannon unless he got a quick and stunning jump on him. He lifted a crippling kick into the groin, and Shannon groaned as he doubled over in pain.

That was the advantage Wiley needed, and all he had to do was to finish it. He raised his knee, locked his hands together, and brought them savagely down against the base of the neck. The brutal force drove the face into his waiting knee. Shannon tried to scream, and the pain in his voice shredded any semblance of words. He fell against Wiley's knee, then slumped to one side.

Wiley stood over him and breathed hard. There was no stirring in Shannon, and he was amazed that he had done such a complete job on him.

He looked up, and the girl was still here. That startled him; he was sure that she would have run at her first chance.

She stared at him in wide-eyed wonder, and somehow that aroused his anger. "Why didn't you run? I'm one of the Americans."

"I know," she said gravely.

He shook his head in exasperation. Didn't she understand that she had been in peril? That the streets were no place for her at night?

With an unexplained perverseness, he tried to arouse the same loathing she must have for the prone figure.

"I'm one of those kind too."

The big-eyed wonder had never left her face. "No, Señor. I do not think so. If I did, wouldn't I have run?"

"Maybe you should have," he growled.

She gave him a flashing smile. "You cannot even make yourself sound like that. Señor, I have not yet thanked you."

That embarrassed him. "You don't have to. But you can make me feel better by letting me see you home."

He thought she was going to refuse, but after a further grave survey, she nodded. "I think I would be grateful." She looked down at Shannon before they started away. "You leave him here?"

"Do you feel a softness for him?" It was odd, but there seemed to be a veiled animosity between them. He saw the expressive movement of her shoulders.

"I do not care what happens to him. Doesn't that surprise you? Didn't you expect that I would want to see him knifed? I am Mexican."

He grinned sheepishly. "I've been told such things."

She stole a glance at him. "And I have been told many bad things about you. The Americanos are murderers, rapists, and robbers."

He gave that a little thought. "I suspect both races have bad people in them. Like that one back there."

She had a delightful smile. It started at the corners of her mouth, then stole across her face. "That could be the answer," she agreed.

"How did you learn to speak English so well?"

Her laughter was the pealing of a bell. "The mistakes I must make. My brother did business with the traders, and he had to learn to keep them—" she broke off and blushed.

"To keep them from cheating him," she went on. "He did not approve of me learning, but I did. We have even had some of the traders in our house for dinner. Perea insisted I give them a formal hospitality. No more."

"I'm glad you talk English." That didn't explain what made him feel so good, but he couldn't put that into words. He couldn't explain it, but he felt on unexpected happiness. It had only happened in the last few seconds.

"It is not far now," she said. She had something else to say that gave her difficulty. "Señor, I cannot ask you in."

"Sure." His voice was rough. He hadn't expected her to say that.

"It is not because I am not grateful," she wailed. "But our customs, my brother . . ."

She stumbled with her explanation, but it lifted the stone off his heart. It was not her wish; it was something she could not help.

"Sure." The gentleness was back in his voice. "I understand. Maybe I can run into you again when you go to the market, or something like that."

"It is possible. Our house is just ahead."

He looked at it in disbelief. It was the first house he and Elam had stopped before, the house with the surrounding walls and its climbing honeysuckle. He remembered the strain of guitar music and the fragrance of the honeysuckle. Was it possible that things worked out this way?

"I remember this house," he cried. "I stopped outside the walls and heard somebody playing a guitar. Was it you?"

Embarrassment touched her face. "It is possible it could have been me." She looked into his face and was caught up in the force of the moment.

"You'd better go in," he said gruffly. "Maybe we'll see each other soon."

He thought she was going to breath a yes, but she turned and hurried through the gate. He heard the dry creaking of its hinges, then she was gone.

He swore at himself. He hadn't even thought to ask her name. It wouldn't make any big difference; he knew where she lived. He could always find out who she was.

Perea Yocupico paced beside the horse and buggy. *Dios*! What was taking Dorsett so long? He was furnishing his newest buggy and best horse, and he had hired Rufino Rocha to drive it for the Americano. Rocha knew the way to Chihuahua City, and he was happy to be hired for the long trip.

Yocupico paced around the buggy. Rocha sat there silent. He was wise enough not to break into Yocupico's thoughts when he was this agitated. The buggy couldn't carry many provisions, but Rocha would know where to purchase food along the way.

Yocupico swore again. It was dark and quiet here. It was just as he had told Dorsett—the gringo general's ball was drawing all the attention. But just the same he wanted to get Dorsett and the woman on their way before somebody happened to see him with them. He shivered as a thought hit him. It would be a bad thing if some connection was established between him, Dorsett, and the rifles. The gringos had a very long nose when it came to smelling out an intrigue. He wanted those rifles for Mexico very badly, but not enough to go up before a firing squad because of them. He pounded a fist into his palm. Why didn't Dorsett come?

He started as he saw the two figures hurrying toward the buggy. A long cloak hid the woman. Yocupico wondered if she was worse. He had thought her not well the last time he saw her. When they stopped before him, he noticed she leaned against Dorsett. She was not better.

"Nearly thirty minutes I have waited," he said crossly. "It is my buggy and horse. I have hired Rufino Rocha to be your driver."

Dorsett smiled faintly. "Good. He's worked for me before. I spent time trying to see Hendricks. But he was at the palace. Tell him where I'm going. I'll get word to him. Don't fail me. It's important."

Yocupico bristled. Did Dorsett think he talked to some peon? He smothered the resentment. Dorsett showed he was under great strain.

Dorsett helped the woman into the buggy, deposited a few pieces of luggage, then turned and thrust out his hand.

Yocupico took it. It was seldom done between them, and it embarrassed him. "*Vaya con Dios*," he muttered.

TWELVE

Suspicion must have been working behind Shannon's battered face, for he came by next day where Wiley was working. He made no verbal accusation, but the one open eye made it for him.

Wiley gave him an audacious grin. Before last night, he would have worried about Shannon's animosity, but not now. Last night was worth it; at least, the fragment of it he had had with her. The next time he got into town he would learn her name, and the anticipation put a luster on this day.

Shannon turned away without opening his mouth. He wouldn't have let it go like that unless he was so uncertain. Wiley grinned after him. He was sorry Shannon's mauling hadn't been worse; the man had earned all of it.

It was the first time in a long while that he felt like whistling, and he tore into the work. Other troopers hooted derisively at him, but he kept on heaving those forty-pound bricks around. He felt like working.

Elam came up to see him and squatted on his heels. "Did you have anything to do with Shannon's face?"

Wiley's look was innocent. "Did something happen to him?"

Elam picked up a handful of sand and threw it away. "Doniphan isn't accusing you, but Buckley thinks you had a hand in it. Shannon looks like a building fell on his face."

"Now, if I ain't right sorry to hear that."

"Doniphan says you couldn't have done it because you can't handle Shannon."

Wiley felt a stab of regret. That was too bad. He couldn't claim credit. "What does Shannon say?"

Elam grinned. "Doniphan says it must be the biggest man in the world, the way Shannon described him."

Wiley had difficulty in keeping his grin from showing. "But you still think Doniphan's wrong?"

Elam stared at him hard. "I'll swear there's times when I can't make you out. I talked to Doniphan a long time this morning. Kearny's loaded him with work. He wants Doniphan to draw up new laws to govern New Mexico."

"Who's better qualified, Daniel?"

"Nobody. But it's a hell of a job. Aleck is calling in Mexican lawyers to help out with any United States officers he can find who have legal experience. He was in a talkative mood. He says he'll wind up with no credit from anybody. That the only thing he would get is yelling at for stepping on everybody's toes."

Wiley was puzzled. "What made him say something like that?"

"First, he has to make the new laws conform

with the United States Constitution. Kearny's given him something to work with, something he calls Kearny's code. Along with that he's got the Missouri statutes, the laws of Texas, and the Livingstone Code. My God, I can sympathize with him. How is one man expected to weave all those together with it coming out making sense to everybody?"

Wiley laughed. "Didn't you offer him your help?"

"I can't make any fun of Aleck, Wiley. He's got a miserable job. The Mexicans have lived under four hundred years of customs, traditions, and laws. Even their food and clothes follow an old, accepted pattern. It won't be easy to change them over in anything."

That erased Wiley's humor. It wasn't hard to understand why Doniphan had talked so long to Elam. Elam was one of the few educated men around.

Elam threw away another handful of sand. "Something else is troubling him. Kearny's talking about getting orders to march to California. He thinks Doniphan's volunteers can handle New Mexico."

He cleared his lungs and spat. "I didn't know Aleck used the kind of language he put on Kearny. He could have a right to be worried. Just because the Mexicans have run so far doesn't mean that they will forever."

Wiley hadn't thought of the Mexicans fighting for quite a while. Damn it! He thought they had given up Santa Fe for good.

He scowled at Elam. "What's Kearny going to California for?"

Elam shrugged. "Aleck didn't talk to me about Kearny's reasons. I'm guessing why. The United States isn't supposed to claim land west of the Rio Grande. The river's been a historic boundary for I don't know how long. But Kearny can't leave Mexicans occupying it; not if he intends to march to California. That would leave a strip of enemy territory in his rear."

Wiley's face showed the effort of trying to handle all these new thoughts. He didn't have enough background to understand them. "It looks to me like we're just out to grab any piece of land we want."

Elam sighed. "I'm not trying to figure any reason for it." He hadn't imparted all of his news. "They're talking about a new revolt all over town."

Wiley stood and stretched to get the kinks out of his muscles. A man's muscles revolted when he tried to put them back to work after a long rest. "Where did you hear that?"

"I heard it from a faro dealer. The Navajos and Apaches are causing trouble."

Wiley cussed. "Didn't Kearny promise to protect the Mexicans?"

"He did, in one of his speeches on the plaza. But he's going without doing anything about it. Doniphan can do that, too."

"Jesus," Wiley said softly. "They're putting everything onto his back, aren't they?"

Elam smiled bleakly. "He's to make contact when he can with the Indians and negotiate a treaty."

"How's he going to do it all, Daniel?"

"He's squirming under it, but he'll handle it."

Buckley was headed this way, and Wiley didn't want him on him for any reason. He lifted the form from a sun-hardened brick. He wouldn't take Doniphan's responsibilities for all the money in the world.

"I'll see you tonight, Daniel."

He placed the brick in its tier and grinned as Buckley put a sour eye on him as he passed. His thought went back to Elam's words. He wanted nothing more to handle than his own piece of ground. His head wasn't big enough to handle any more. He spent a lot of time the rest of the day, thinking about Doniphan. He wondered what drove some men and couldn't arouse others. He felt a vague irritation. Sometimes he couldn't help but feel left out of things.

Santa Fe was seven thousand feet in altitude, and the morning air had a sharp bite to it. He didn't think he would care for a Santa Fe winter.

He still worked on the fort, and he was getting damned tired of it. He guessed Doniphan had forgotten all about him. He rarely saw him anymore, and that was no surprise, not with the load of work dumped on Doniphan's back. Elam didn't talk about it anymore. Wiley was just as relieved that Elam didn't have something new to tell him. He didn't want to be drawn into it in any way. All he wanted to do was to put in the time he had to put in and take care of his personal business.

He had looked for Dorsett on the few passes he had received, and he had begun to wonder if his heart wasn't in it like it had been. What he really wanted to do was to find Maria and talk to her again. Yes, he knew her name. He had stood outside the wall and asked passers-by until he found one who spoke English. The man who lived in the *casa* behind the wall was Perea Yocupico and his sister was Maria. No, their parents had died several years ago, and Perea looked after his sister.

The man had had something on his mind, and he had been afraid to say it.

"Go ahead," Wiley had said. He wanted any scrap of information he could get.

"Señor, I do not think Don Perea will accept an Americano's call on his house."

Wiley had grinned wryly. He had no doubt of that. He didn't need the warning; he knew enough about their customs.

He had seen Maria twice after that. Once, with

her brother at the market, and another time with a female companion. He hadn't dared approach her the first time. He could just imagine what Yocupico's reaction would be. That Yocupico was a cold fish. His eyes had really seen nothing. They had touched on Wiley and moved on without seeing him. It made him angry and uncomfortable at the same time.

The second time, he had dared to step out before her. Her eyes sparkled before she could compose her face. Her female companion said something in fierce Spanish, and Maria had waved her back.

Maria flashed him a quick look before dropping her eyes again. "My aunt," she said. "It is not proper that I talk to you here." That delightful peal of laughter bubbled up to her lips. "Or at any time, for that matter."

"Maria, I've been hoping to see you again."

She could use her eyes. Each glance battered at Wiley and left him more defenseless. He remembered her as beautiful the night he had pulled her clear of Shannon, but not like this.

Her astonishment showed. "How did you know my name?"

"That didn't take any great ability." He grinned, tickled that he had surprised her. "I knew where you lived. I waited outside your gate until somebody passed by. I had to keep asking until somebody talked English. I asked him."

"And I do not know your name," she murmured.

"Wiley. Wiley Anderson."

She repeated the name, giving it an inflection that made him laugh. "Wiley," she repeated. "It is an odd name. But pleasant."

She looked back, and her aunt was making frantic motions to her. "I must go now. Already, I have scandalized the entire city. If Perea should hear of it . . ." she shivered.

He was concerned for her and angry at her brother. "Are you afraid of your brother?"

"Yes," she admitted. "When I do something that gives me reason to be."

"But will I see you again?"

"I do not know, Señor." She looked full into his eyes. She could not hide the honesty in them. "I hope so."

It seemed as though their eyes met forever, then she was gone. He stared after the pair until they were out of sight. By the way the aunt's head bobbed toward Maria, Wiley had no doubt that she harangued Maria every step of the way. Her family would not approve of him, and he couldn't care less. It was only what she felt that was important to him.

It hit him with a cruel, smashing blow. He had no right to such thoughts. He swore at himself. He had seen her three times, exchanged a few words, and he couldn't be falling in love with her. He groaned in anguish. Even if it was so, he had no right to be thinking about it. He was a married man, and nothing could change that.

People, passing him, looked curiously at him. His torment must be showing on his face.

He had pushed the thoughts of Linda to the back of his mind. Maybe he had hoped that that would make them go away. He had had a different outlook on everything since the first night he had seen Maria. He tried to deny it, but this was the moment to face things honestly. He hadn't even looked for Dorsett very hard. He had told himself that Dorsett was gone from Santa Fe by now. He didn't know whether or not it was true, but he hadn't spent very much effort trying to prove it one way or another.

What did he do now? Try to see Maria at every opportunity? He shook his head. These people looked on marriage differently. Wiley didn't think he had ever heard of them separating. But Maria had to know just how he stood. He smothered his groan at the thought of having to face her and tell her what she must know.

He stared in the direction she had disappeared. If he had the chance, he would like to tell her today and get it off his mind. He wished he could go to her house and knock for admittance. That wouldn't do at all; he might run into Yocupico. If Yocupico knew what was in Wiley's mind, he would shoot him for even looking at his sister.

He turned back toward camp, and his face was set in white grimness.

THIRTEEN

Wiley wangled every pass he could get. He knew his chances to see Maria at night were almost nil, and he argued with Buckley that he wouldn't ask for night passes if Buckley would let him go in a few times in the daytime. Buckley was stubborn. A couple of times Wiley had to go over his head to ask Doniphan. He was startled to see how worn Doniphan looked.

"Do you feel bad, Aleck?"

Doniphan rubbed his eyes. "No worse than usual, Wiley." He gestured at the paper-littered table in his tent. "My God, it's unbelievable that the army insists on documenting everything a man does."

"I guess it's pure hell," Wiley said sympathetically. "Are things getting any better?"

"Each morning I swear today has to be better than yesterday, and it only gets worse. The Navajos grow more bold in their raids, and they're terrorizing the Mexicans. The little villages can't put up much defense, and the Mexicans are demanding we protect them from the raids."

That outraged Wiley. "Only a short time ago they were against us. Now they're hollering at us to protect them."

Doniphan's smile didn't have much strength. "It's natural enough, Wiley. We took over their country and promised them peace and protection. We scattered their army, and we're expected to take its place. It's up to us to deliver, Wiley."

"Damned if you don't work things around, Aleck. I wouldn't see it that way."

That pulled a weak laugh from Doniphan. "Do you have something special on your mind, Wiley?"

"Buckley isn't around, and I'd sure like to go into town. If it wouldn't bother you too much . . ."

Doniphan studied him with that quick glint in his eyes. "Planning more trouble, Wiley?"

"Aw, Aleck. I haven't been in trouble for a long time. I've been working steady on the fort."

Doniphan's smile softened his face. "I'm aware of that, Wiley. I think you've worked on it long enough."

Wiley sighed in pure pleasure. "I'm glad to hear that. And I'd sure appreciate getting out of that mud."

"How would you like to go on a trip with me, Wiley? I've got to ride out and try to reason with the Navajos."

"You mean just you and me?" Wiley's face showed quick alarm.

Doniphan's laughter was unrepressed this time. "Colonel Price will have the Second Missourians in Santa Fe in a few days. He'll protect it while the First Missourian marches off to see if we can get this Navajo mess cleaned up."

This was the excuse Wiley needed to tell Maria why he couldn't see her any more. Maybe he was giving himself undue credit in believing that a feeling was building in her too. But this would squash it. Sure it hurt to think he wouldn't see her again. A man just let himself drift into the damndest messes without realizing it. Dorsett wasn't in Santa Fe, Wiley was positive of that. But ever since Maria Yocupico had crowded into his head, he hadn't had much room for anything else. He might as well be riding with the First Missourians as doing anything else.

"I think I'd like that, Aleck."

"Good." Doniphan scribbled out the pass. "Take as much time as you want."

Wiley's face was reflective as he walked into Santa Fe. He didn't know how he was going to contact her. He couldn't just pound on her gate. He would have to wait outside until she came through it. It was going to be a hard thing to tell her he was leaving. He would see some hurt in her eyes, but this was turning out the best for both of them.

He stood across the street from the gate and waited. What if she didn't come out today? He frowned. He didn't want to think about that.

People drifted down the street, and all of them put curious eyes on him. Several youngsters came by, and they gave him a wide berth. A thought occurred to him; he might get one of them to go to the Yocupico house and ask for Maria. His face brightened. Something might be worked out of that, if he could make one of the kids understand.

He took a step toward the next kid, and the kid's eyes widened in instant alarm. Another step sent the kid off in wild flight. Wiley sighed. There went a no-good idea. He doubted there was a kid in Santa Fe who hadn't been taught by its parents to fear the Americanos. He thought with painful humor, I haven't eaten a kid since I've been here.

He shifted his weight. Just standing around put an ache in a man's legs about as quick as anything he knew. He wished he could talk to somebody about Maria, but he didn't have a soul to listen to him. At his first word about her, they would jump to the wrong conclusion. They would frown at him, or make him squirm under ribald remarks. He couldn't stand that at all.

A buggy came down the street, and Wiley was struck by the weary appearance of the horse. It barely lifted its hoofs, and its head drooped low. That animal had been on a long, wearing trip.

The buggy was caked with dust, and the driver showed the same kind of wear. Wiley's eyes left him, then came back. It was difficult for him to distinguish between Mexicans, but he knew that one. That was the one he had caught trying to get into the traders' camp, and he was almost certain he had seen him the night he had chased Dorsett.

The buggy turned the corner, and Wiley trailed it, his mind picking at several conclusions. Had this Mexican driven Dorsett out of Santa Fe? If so, it had been a long way. The appearance of the buggy and horse fitted that. Why would Dorsett want a buggy? Could it be because it made for more comfortable traveling with a woman? That could mean Linda, and everything seemed to fit it.

He had no trouble keeping up with the horse and buggy. Maybe now he could get some answers. He opened his mouth to yell at the driver, but the man turned in at the carriage entrance in the side wall.

Wiley stopped and frowned. He had seen the shabby clothes; this wasn't the kind of guest the Yocupicos invited to their home. Had Yocupico hired the Mexican to drive Dorsett out of Santa Fe? The questions were beginning to pile up. This was a new string dangling from the tangled mass. He had to pull on it; it was the only one offered him.

He waited beside the carriage entrance and, through its bars, he caught an occasional glimpse of a servant. He didn't see Maria or her brother or the driver of the buggy.

A good half hour passed before the driver came

out. He shuffled, and his shoulders sagged. Deep fatigue had etched his face. He wouldn't have seen Wiley, if Wiley hadn't stopped him.

Wiley seized him by the shoulder. There wasn't much flesh covering the bony structure. "Where did you take Dorsett?"

That random shot hit; he could tell by the startled alarm that filled the Mexican's face. "Señor." He went into a rapid streak of Spanish. Wiley could manage to catch only a word or two out of it.

His fingers bit harder. "Señor Dorsett. And the Señora. *Donde*?"

The Mexican understood what he heard; it registered in his face. Stubbornness filled his eyes, and he repeatedly shook his head. "*No comprendo*."

It made Wiley wild. This man knew what he was talking about. How was he going to get it out of him?

He shook him in savage desperation, and the Mexican howled. That was bad. It was going to attract a crowd, but Wiley couldn't help it. All the man had to do was to tell him where he had taken Dorsett and Linda.

He could try to batter it out of him with his fists, but this was an old man. He backed him up against the wall and pinned him there with his weight.

"Dorsett and the Señora," he repeated. He

would hold him here until the man understood there was no other way of being set free.

He slammed his elbow under the man's chin with enough force to click his teeth. He howled again when Wiley threateningly raised the elbow again.

A couple of people stopped across the street. "*Vaya*," Wiley yelled at them. He didn't want a crowd gathering. His yell and scowl didn't faze them.

The man bawled something at them, and Wiley thought it might be a plea for help. Wouldn't that be a mess, if they tried it? He didn't want to fight a bunch of Mexicans.

"Why are you holding Rocha, Señor?"

The voice came from behind Wiley, and it made him jump. He jerked his head around and stared into the cold, haughty face of Perea Yocupico. The man was dressed fancy this morning in black velvet and Cordovan leather.

He let go of Rocha. He doubted Rocha would run as long as Yocupico was here.

"Señor, it's important to me. I want to know where he drove that buggy." Understanding hit Wiley. Rocha would never have been able to afford anything like that buggy and horse. It had to be Yocupico who had furnished them. Then Yocupico knew where Dorsett and Linda had gone.

"Where did Dorsett and the woman go?"

Yocupico did a good job of keeping his face blank, but he couldn't help keep the flicker of emotion out of his eyes. Wiley knew a fierce elation. Yocupico knew.

Yocupico shrugged. "*No comprendo*."

Wiley's face flamed. Did the man take him for a damned dummy? The first thing Yocupico had said had been in good English. "You talked English well enough a couple of seconds ago."

A tinge of color washed Yocupico's face. By implication, Wiley was calling him a liar.

Rocha hurled a stream of Spanish words at him, and Yocupico snapped something at him. Wiley knew Yocupico was telling him to shut up.

Yocupico's eyes were filled with hating. "I do not know what you're talking about, Señor."

He put his hand on Rocha's arm, and Wiley knew what was in his mind. He was going to pull Rocha clear of this.

"And I say you're a damned liar."

That put a murderous glint in Yocupico's eyes and whitened his lips. "You do not know what you're saying, Señor. I forgive you this once." He pulled on Rocha's arm.

Wiley's frustration made him frantic. Again he was so close, and a door was slamming in his face.

He sprang forward to block Yocupico's way. "You know where Dorsett is. You're not leaving until you tell me where he went."

Yocupico's breathing made a harsh, rasping sound, and his eyes were black, hating pools. More people were gathering, and that made Wiley more uncomfortable. But he had no intention of letting Yocupico go.

"If this is the way you want it," Yocupico hissed. A knife flashed into his hand, and he jumped at Wiley.

He almost caught Wiley unawares. He twisted his upper body, and the blade slid across his arm. It didn't cut, but it ripped the sleeve of his uniform. The closeness popped sweat out on Wiley's forehead.

His hands fastened on the extended wrist, and he wrenched and levered on it. The knife clattered to the ground, and Yocupico yelped in pain.

Wiley took one hand off the wrist and made a fist of it. With the other hand he jerked Yocupico in close to him. "All right," he said. "This is the way you wanted it."

He clubbed Yocupico on the hinge of the jaw, an angry blow with momentum and power behind it. It knocked the sense out of Yocupico, and he slumped to the ground.

Wiley rubbed his fist. He was sorry it had turned out this way; he hadn't intended hitting Yocupico, but a knife always scared him.

He didn't have time to explain it to Rocha. The man jumped on his back and wrapped his arms around his neck. He must have thought he was riding a horse, the way his heels tried to dig into Wiley's ribs.

"Why, you damned fool," Wiley roared. With Rocha's yelling, he could hardly make himself heard.

The Mexicans poured across the street. They came in a solid wave, and they rolled over him. They swarmed him under by sheer numbers and, as he went down, he thought dully, I must have hit one who is important to them.

FOURTEEN

Wiley had seen Doniphan angry before, but this was the zenith. He thought for a moment Doniphan was going to hit him; he knew he certainly wanted to.

"I can't believe it." Doniphan's tone attested to that. "The first thing you do when you get into town is to start another riot. I bend over backward to keep the peace here, and you stir up trouble. You have a positive genius for it."

Wiley couldn't look him in the eyes. He hadn't intended what had happened, but it seemed a normal build-up he couldn't stop. It was a good thing Doniphan's volunteers were in town and heard the noise. If they hadn't stopped it, Wiley didn't know where he would be. He didn't know how many Mexicans had him down and were kicking and pounding him.

Every time he got halfway back to his feet, another blow or kick would send him back down. He was an aching mass of bruises and contusions, and the smallest effort of movement made him want to yelp. Maybe he was lucky to come out of it at all.

"Not only did you start a riot, but you picked out a member of the most influential family in town to attack. Will you give me one reason why?"

Wiley had one, but he didn't think Doniphan would accept it. All he had wanted was that Yocupico tell him where Dorsett was, and the man had pulled a knife on him. Yocupico's reaction was proof to Wiley that he knew Dorsett's whereabouts. So did the one called Rocha. He wondered what Yocupico would tell Maria about it. He would tell her something, but probably not the truth. It made Wiley sick to think of what her opinion of him must be.

"Haven't you got anything at all to say about it?"

Wiley shook his head. What he could say about it wouldn't do him any good.

"You're a troublemaker, Wiley." There was more sorrow than outrage in Doniphan's voice. "I can't afford you anymore. I've got too much on my hands as it is. I'm transferring you to Price's Second Missourians when he gets here. I'm recommending to him that he keep you working on Fort Marcy for his own peace of mind."

Wiley's eyes were sick. That would take away every friend he had. Just being in the volunteers was tough enough without isolation.

"Don't do that, Aleck," he pleaded. "Let me go with you. I promise I won't get in any more trouble."

"That was your last promise. I think the trouble you're getting into is tied up with your personal problems. Can you promise me you've solved that?"

Wiley couldn't. If he ran across Dorsett, he would do something about him. If he went with the First Missourians, he didn't expect to see Dorsett again. But he couldn't promise Doniphan that. He kept his mouth shut.

Doniphan sighed. "I thought not, Wiley. One thing I can say for you; you're not a liar. I'll have the transfer made out in a couple of days."

Wiley stood among the Second Missourians and watched Doniphan and the First ride out. It wasn't the same. He still might be among Missourians, but it wasn't Clay County men. Doniphan didn't look at him as he led off the column. A lot of the men grinned and waved at him. Elam kept twisting around in the saddle to look back at him, and his face was woebegone. Wiley watched the column until distance diminished it to a thin wavery line. He had never felt so lonely.

"Are you going to stand there all day?" a sergeant bawled.

Buckley used to yell at him too, but there was a difference. Buckley might not care for him, but he knew him. This sergeant couldn't have picked him out from a post. Wiley's feet dragged toward Fort Marcy. His heart was getting too heavy for a man to carry around with him.

He was rebellious and angry toward Doniphan,

and he couldn't work it off. When he couldn't stand it anymore, he would simply walk off of the job. He knew what it would be called, and he had a new dislike for the word. A long time back he had faced it without it bothering him. It did now. He worried about what Elam and the others thought of him, and he had a big concern over the way Doniphan had looked at him. He had another thing that kept pricking at him. What did Maria think of him now? She could have only scorn for him, and that hurt. When he decided to leave the army, he would try to see her before he left Santa Fe. Maybe he would never be able to explain it to her satisfaction, but perhaps he might soften her eyes a little.

At night he was too damned tired to think much of anything, and he didn't want to. He tried to keep his accusation built up, and it weakened on him. He had a right to be resentful of Doniphan; Doniphan hadn't given him much of a shake. That was the thought he wanted to hold on to, and it was as slippery as a wet bar of soap. That was when his treacherous thoughts betrayed him. He hadn't given Doniphan much of a shake either.

He didn't talk much to the Second Missourians, and they didn't seem to care one way or the other. This wasn't his outfit, and nothing he or they could do would make it the same. He couldn't help but overhear scraps of conversation. Doniphan was riding out to meet the Navajos for treaty talk, and nobody envied him the job. The damned commissary wagons were failing again to get through. That was probably true. The food situation wasn't very good in Santa Fe. It must be pure hell out there on Doniphan's route. Somebody said he hadn't taken more than parched corn and not an abundant supply of that. When they ran out of parched corn, what would they eat? They wouldn't find much to live off in this Godforsaken country.

It increased Wiley's feeling of guilt. Damn it, he hadn't asked to stay here. All he wanted to do was to be marching with the First Missourians.

The dreary days of November piled up, and Wiley had advance warning that this could be brutal country in wintertime. Ice formed in the water buckets, and the air was snapping cold. Price let up on Wiley, and he went into town for the first time in a month. He wandered listlessly about the streets and knew there was little chance of seeing Maria. But he stood out in front of that wall for a while. He admitted there might be some danger in it. Yocupico might still remember that blow. More important, he might be determined to pay it back.

He went back to camp early, and his blankets weren't enough to turn the chill. He lay there, staring up into the blackness. He was without a purpose, and for the first time he realized how aimless it left a man. As long as he was looking for Dorsett and Linda, it had filled him with determination. Now he just didn't have anything to fill its void. He remembered how violent his hating had been. Where had that gone? Hating for the sake of a target, he thought dully. If he knew where to look for Dorsett, it would come back. He rolled over and tried to pull the blankets more tightly about him. What was he doing here? He asked that question every night and never came up with a suitable answer.

He got another day to go into town the end of the month. Many of the Mexicans wore serapes, a blanket with a hole cut for the head in its center. The snap in the day drove any listless movement out of them.

He stopped by Maria's wall for a little while, but a man didn't stand around too long in this weather. He thought of something to eat, and today could relish the heat of chili and tamales. He walked toward the market area, and there was a new quickness in people. Maybe after he had some food he would have a couple of drinks of Taos Lightning. He had no money in his pockets; the army hadn't been paid for six months. Even the eighteen cents a day was only a paper promise. But he could beat the lack of pay. All of the buttons on his coat were intact. He had enough buttons to get started, at least, on a good drunk.

He turned around, took a step, and bumped squarely into Maria.

"Maria!" The tone he gave her name showed the elation in his heart.

He had never seen her look better. She wore a much heavier mantilla, wool, he guessed, and it reached to her ankles. It was gaily striped, and her eyes picked up the colors. The cold had crimsoned her cheeks, and the sight of him seemed to increase it.

She took control of her feelings. She could turn those expressive features into a frozen block of ice.

"Do not touch me." She moved back before his extended hand.

He looked guilty as he retrieved the hand. That had been instinctive. "Maria, I didn't mean to . . ."

She had some of the haughtiness of her brother, and she could use it more brutally than a club. "I do not want even to speak to you again."

He knew why, but he had to ask her; he had to hear her say it. "But why, Maria?"

She had a blending of scorn and contempt to mix into the haughtiness. "Because you knocked my brother down for no reason at all." Each word put her farther away from him.

"Is that what he told you?"

"You were beating Rufino Rocha. Perea tried to save him. You turned to him."

He wished he could swear. He didn't know how he was going to do it, but he had to make her listen to the true account, even if it made him tell her everything. It made him sick to think of shock and hurt growing in her face, but that would be better than what she thought now.

He seized her wrist, ignoring her indignation. "Maria, you've got to listen to me." He had to get her out of the traffic before the stalls, and he tugged on her wrist. He felt the resistance. If it grew worse, he couldn't stop her.

"Please," he begged.

Her eyes studied his face, then turned uncertain. "I will listen. For only a second or two."

He drew her across the street and around a corner. The wind couldn't get at them here. He didn't even know where to start. He took a deep breath and plunged in.

"Maria, I came to Santa Fe. To find a man—and a woman."

The latter startled her. She moistened her lips. "What woman?"

"My wife," he said in little more than a whisper.

She stared at him as though she didn't understand, then she winced. "Your wife?"

He nodded miserably. He sketched over his marriage and Linda's flight with Dorsett. "I heard they came to Santa Fe. Then the war broke out. The only way I could get here was to join up."

"You must have loved her very much."

He stared at her in astonishment. "Love her? I hated her and Dorsett. I lived to catch up with them. I knew I was going to kill him. I wasn't certain what I was going to do with her."

A shiver ran through her. "It must be very bad to hate like that."

"Yes," he said grimly. "I saw my man one night here. I almost caught up with him, but he lost me."

He had erected a new barrier between them. It was in her eyes. "I do not see where any of this touches me."

"Rufino Rocha was with Dorsett that night."

Her mouth was an O. "Señor Dorsett. Is he the man you hunt?"

"You know him?"

"He has been to our home a few times. He and Perea are in something together. Once, he had a woman with him."

"You've seen her? A blonde woman?"

She nodded mutely. "She didn't look well."

He didn't know about that. He felt no pity and didn't expect to.

Now he could say to her that her brother was a liar; with her own eyes she knew that there was some connection between Rocha, Dorsett, and her brother. "I had to tell you, Maria, why I really came to Santa Fe. Even though I knew it would end my seeing you."

He thought that was a film of tears in her eyes, though she looked away too quickly for him to be sure.

"Maria, can't you see? Something was happening to me that I didn't expect. And I couldn't let it. I owed that to both of us."

She twisted a fold of the mantilla between her fingers. "I do not understand. You did nothing that you could be blamed for."

A twisted grin was the best he could do. "No. But something was building up that scared me. In fairness to you, I had to tell you. All I could do was wait for you to come out. Rocha drove a tired horse and mud-caked buggy into your entrance. I told you I saw Rocha with Dorsett. I thought maybe he had driven Dorsett away from Santa Fe. I was trying to make Rocha admit it when your brother stopped me."

Her eyes flashed. "Perea lied to me. He knew what you were trying to make Rocha tell you."

"He knew. I saw it in his face."

"Perea sent Dorsett and your wife—" that word came hard for her, "away in our buggy. Rocha drove it."

He felt limp with relief. At least she believed him, and maybe her hating would not be so great. "Where did Rocha take him, Maria?"

"I think I heard Perea say Chihuahua City. I am not certain. Maybe that was about something else. But I do know he has a deal with Dorsett that is driving him crazy. Whatever it is, he cannot complete, and it is making a different man of him."

Wiley didn't care what Yocupico's deal with Dorsett was. That was their affair. But Dorsett's destination was his business.

He wished he could say all of the things that swelled into his heart. He had seen her only a few times, and yet she had grown to mean so much to him.

"Maria, I wish I could show you my country someday. Most of the year it is green, and it is a gentler country than this one."

She couldn't stop the tears from spilling out of her eyes. "I think I would like to see it, Wiley."

His grin at the pronunciation of his name hurt him. "I hope I can see you again, Maria."

"*Vaya con Dios*, Wiley." She ducked her head, whipped around, and was suddenly running down the street.

He didn't know a man's heart could hurt so much. He thought it had hurt when Linda left him. He knew now that it hadn't at all. His pride had been bruised, and in his blindness he had called it something else. His face brightened as the thought filtered into his mind. If he found Dorsett and Linda and gave them his permission to go without fear, would it change things? He didn't know what laws they had about marriage in Mexico, but there ought to be some way a man and woman could be legally separated. Would it change things in Maria's eyes? He didn't know about that. He could only go ahead and see how things developed. He was sure of one thing; this put him on a brighter road than the one he had been traveling.

FIFTEEN

Wiley had only a vague idea of where Chihuahua City lay. He had learned that first he would reach Padilla on the Rio Grande River some seventy miles below Santa Fe. Many miles ago he had quit looking behind him. A couple of nights ago he had slipped the claybank off the picket line and eased out of the camp. He had all the food he could scrounge and a little corn for the claybank. Padilla was supposed to be a town of several hundred people; he hoped to buy more food for himself and the horse there. "Buy" was a carelessly used term; he had nothing in his pockets. He would have to trade for what he needed. He hoped some of the equipment was worth bartering. But he might as well quit worrying about it until he reached Padilla.

He should reach Padilla sometime around dark. He hoped he would find somebody there who could speak English. The deeper he got into this country, the bigger the headache of communication.

He passed a couple of Mexicans, trudging behind their firewood-laden burros. He must be closer to the town than he thought. He tried to talk to them, and they shook their heads at every word. He couldn't string enough Spanish together to get across to them.

He gave up and pushed the horse on past them. He heard one of them call him a *Los Goddamie* and grinned wryly. He had been called that often enough to know what it meant. It was derived from the American's use of his favorite oath.

The winter darkness seemed to come all at once. He saw campfires blink into flame, dotting the land ahead of him. He frowned at the winking red eyes. Who could be camping out like this? He had left Price in Santa Fe. Doniphan? He dismissed that. Doniphan was somewhere in the mountains, trying to talk to the Navajos. It left only the Mexicans to camp in this force, and he felt his stomach knot. He had better take every precaution until he knew for sure.

He pulled the claybank off of the road and eased through the brush. He wouldn't dare ride much farther, and he hated the thought of going on foot. He could easily get lost in this strange country.

The fires grew bigger, and he saw occasional figures pass before them. Something was all wrong, and he couldn't figure out what it was. He had better tie the horse and sneak up closer.

He started to swing down, and the voice, coming out of the black, put a gripping shock on him. "Hold it right there, mister, or I'll put a hole in you."

Wiley shook inwardly. Had he run into a bandit's camp? But nobody down here could speak with that unmistakable Missouri twang.

"I'm holding right steady," he said. "Who are you?"

"You better give out some information first."

"Wiley Anderson. The First Missourians." It occurred to him that he wasn't of the First anymore, but he still thought of himself that way.

"The hell it is." The figure detached itself from the shadow of a bush and came toward him. "Hell, Wiley. Don't you know Ben Marshall?"

Wiley swallowed hard. He couldn't believe it until Marshall got almost up to him. The thought flashed through his mind that Marshall had deserted too. But that couldn't be. He was out here with a rifle, like he was on sentry duty, and there were all those campfires up ahead.

"Ben, who's that outfit?"

Marshall shook his head as though he suspected Wiley's sanity. "Who else would I be on sentry duty for? You ought to know who it is. You were with it long enough before you transferred."

That stung Wiley. "I didn't have anything to do with it," he snapped. "Doniphan got sore at me."

"You gotta see him again," Marshall said decisively. "He'll want to know what you're doing down here."

Wiley didn't want to see him at all. The best he could get out of it was to be sent back to Santa Fe. He tried to argue Marshall out of it, but he couldn't budge him. Something had happened in the past few weeks to change Marshall. He seemed to have put on some age in a hurry.

He wished he could hammer Marshall's head. What was Doniphan doing down here anyway?

He put it into words, and Marshall said, "We get the rumor we're on our way to join up with General Wood in Chihuahua City. There's all kind of reports that a dozen Mexican armies are blocking our way." He spat with a new authority. "I'd just like to see them do it."

That put a new light on everything. If any part of Marshall's report was true, Wiley was a damned fool to think he could get to Chihuahua City alone. But he could reach it as part of Doniphan's army—if he could talk him into it.

He led the claybank and plodded ahead of Marshall.

"How come you changed all of a sudden?" Marshall asked with suspicious curiosity. "One moment you're arguing like hell, and the next you ain't got a word to say."

Wiley shrugged. "I saw it wasn't any use with you." His mind was busy. He didn't know what he was going to say to Doniphan. He wondered if it would be better to tell Doniphan everything. He discarded that. With everything Doniphan had on his hands, he wouldn't appreciate Wiley just driving ahead on his own aims. That had outraged Doniphan before. He sighed as he got deeper into the mental morass. He would just have to see how it turned out.

Marshall marched him down the company street. Every time he passed a campfire, somebody recognized and yelled at him. He shook hands and took whacks on the back. His mouth worked; they had missed him.

He shook hands hard with Elam. "Maybe I can talk to you later. Right now, I've got to see Doniphan."

"You in trouble with him again?" Elam asked in quick alarm.

"I don't know." Wiley couldn't hide the worry in his voice.

"Come back if you can, Wiley. The supply wagons got here. We've got plenty to eat for a change. Hell, we even got our back pay." Disgust wrinkled his face. "And no place to spend it."

Wiley's laugh was weak. Damned if he wouldn't give anything he had to be able to come back here.

He stepped into Doniphan's tent ahead of Marshall. Marshall had a broad grin. "Aleck, look what I found wandering around out in the brush."

Doniphan was dumbfounded. "I don't believe it. I'm seeing things."

Wiley's grin was pretty feeble. "Hello, Aleck."

"How did you get here?"

Doniphan had a sharp nose for a lie; Wiley had

better keep it as near the truth as he could, or Doniphan would throw him out again.

"Aleck, I like to lost my mind working on those walls. I didn't know anybody. The days kept piling up until I couldn't stand it anymore. One night, I just took out, hoping I could catch up with you." He was sorry that Doniphan looked so bad. Those mountains must have been rough on him.

His mouth opened in amazement. Doniphan was laughing until the tears filled his eyes. "You deserted Price to join up with me? That's ironic, Wiley. I'm sending for him, asking him to catch up with us at Valverde. And you risk the charge of desertion to beat him here!" His eyes turned fierce. "Do you know how serious that is?"

Wiley gulped. If he had only a vague idea, Doniphan's expression strengthened it. His face and voice pleaded. "Colonel, I only wanted to get back."

Doniphan wearily shook his head. "We've got fighting ahead of us. I'll need every man. But if you let me down once more—" he sighed and broke off. "I never really reached you before. I don't know what makes me think I can now. Are you hungry?" he asked abruptly.

Wiley grinned. "I traveled pretty light."

"The supplies came through. I guess we can draw rations for another man. I'll get Buckley on the paper work. He'll have to mark you as returned to duty from detached duty. That will stop everybody looking for you as a deserter."

"Thank you, Colonel." Wiley saluted smartly and turned. He had never meant either thing more.

He sat beside the fire with Elam, and his belly was comfortably full. It was time to talk. Elam surprised him by handing him a chew of tobacco. He didn't know Elam chewed and guessed that it was a habit newly picked up. The sweet smell of molasses filled his nostrils as he gnawed off a chew.

Elam smiled. "I'm doing a lot of things I used not to do. But there were times out there when a man craved a chew of tobacco. Rough days, Wiley."

Shannon and Marshall came by and joined them. Even Buckley came along and hunkered down. Wiley felt a sudden envy he didn't quite understand. Some bond had been formed on that Indian trip, something that tied them together. He was shut out, and he could feel the barrier as though he actually ran his hands over it.

"Tell me about it," he said.

Elam looked around, and their nods selected him to do the talking. His eyes had a distant look, and his face had a new hardening that Wiley hadn't seen before.

"A man never knows himself, Wiley, until he comes up against a tough question. This was tough enough. We started out in winter without enough food or adequate clothes. Most of our time we spent cussing the quartermaster. The horses were starved, galled, and mangy. Those mountains made infantry out of a lot of us before we got out of them. That jagged talus wore out our boots, and we were lucky to get moccasins to replace them."

Wiley looked around at the faces. Their absorbed looks said they relived what Elam related. The experience had molded them in the same form and finished it off with a fine detail. He felt that loneliness again, a shut-outedness that he couldn't quite describe.

"I never saw weather turn worse, Wiley. The wind threw snow in our faces with such a force that it felt like sand. The canyons choked with it until it was waist-deep. We kept moving up higher. We welcomed any timber to break the wind. We went through aspens, alders, and piñons. Don't think we didn't hate to climb out of them. As long as they were around we could have a fire. It got so high that a man's joints ached and his nose bled. It turned into a full-fledged blizzard, and it took us twenty hours to get out of it. On top there was no protection, and the wind roared like cannon. It was strong enough to make the horses stagger and lose their footing. A horse screams like a man when it goes over a cliff."

He picked up a stick and drew an aimless

design in the sand. "Doniphan kept yelling for us to keep our hands and faces covered. Every man hated him. I think cursing him kept us going. He had to cajole, threaten, and kick at us to get us going. But he got us through those mountains."

He was silent for a long moment, staring into the fire. "He's quite a man, Wiley."

Wiley stirred irritably. All right. He was ready to admit that. "Go on."

"He led us right into that Navajo camp. Those Indians were mean-looking customers. I wasn't the only one who was scared. If Doniphan was, it didn't show."

Shannon chuckled. "Tell him about those women, Dan. If they weren't the ugliest things I ever saw."

Elam chuckled. "They wore buckskin dresses and white cotton leggings. Their hair was matted and dirty, and they smelled worse than a hog pen." He looked over at Marshall. "Even Ben was satisfied to keep clear of them."

Marshall snorted. "Don't you think I ever learn anything?"

"But those women fed us. I never tasted anything better." His face had a happy remembrance. "Roasted corn and mutton so greasy it ran up to your elbows. But that was eating."

They all remembered it, and Wiley felt more shut out than ever. "Did Doniphan have any trouble getting the treaty signed?"

Elam laughed "He had them treating him like long lost relations. Doniphan won't admit it was quite a job. He says our main job is up ahead. He's had reports that several Mexican armies are between us and Chihuahua City. That's going to be bad for those Mex armies. Because Doniphan is determined to join up with General Wood."

The firelight played on the harsh planes and angles of Wiley's face. He remembered his first, worried estimates of Mexican soldiers. It couldn't touch him now. He had rubbed shoulders with the Mexican people, and he hadn't seen anything to put a fear in a man's head. Maybe he was hankering to join in a little action; maybe he wanted to earn a little respect from these men.

"I'm glad to be back," he said.

Buckley stood. "I wonder if you'll be saying that later. Aleck told me to put you back on the roster."

Buckley's sourness tickled Elam. "He can't get into any trouble around here."

"I wonder," Buckley said and wandered off.

The fire was burning low, and Marshall made the offer to get some more fuel. "I'll get some more wood."

Wiley exchanged looks with Elam after he left. "He's made quite a change."

Shannon stuffed his cheek full of chew. "He ain't a bad kid at all."

Wiley shook his head. The outfit he had marched away with from Leavenworth was gone. A man wouldn't believe that so much change could be brought out in people.

SIXTEEN

The road leading south from Padilla was rutted and bumpy. In the morning light, Wiley could see how many of the First Missourians were afoot. They had paid a frightful toll in horses in the mountains. It was a small miracle that there had been no human cost.

Some of the freighters were carrying army supplies, and it looked good to see them back there. Wiley could remember times when the column didn't have a wagon behind him. But all of those wagons weren't carrying army supplies, and he asked about them.

"The traders are trickling out of Santa Fe," Elam said. "The trading was so poor back there they almost starved to death. The rest of them will catch up with us in Valverde." His smile had a grim cast. "They cuss us, but they want our protection to Chihuahua City."

That put guilt in Wiley. He couldn't see where he was doing anything so different from the traders. He spat between his teeth. Damn it. He would earn that protection before he was through.

He wanted to see Dorsett and Linda, but the driving malice was gone. If he could get a message to them, it might do just as well. All he wanted to tell Linda was that all she had to do was to ask for her freedom. It was surprising how lighthearted it made him. If Hendricks was with the traders, maybe he would take the message to Dorsett and Linda.

He pulled out of the column and dropped back to the following wagons. The Conestagas were big wagons, sixteen feet long. They took up an awkward space, but they could carry a payload of two tons. All of them sagged in the belly so that if the cargo shifted, it would be toward the middle and not break out the endgate. The wagons showed the sign of hard usage. Some of the Osnaberg sheeting was ripped and torn, and the wind flapped it against the bows. The traders were running out of little necessities, such as wheel dope. The grind of the undoped gum hubs grated at a man's nerves. The constant rattle of the linchpins was an additional irritant.

Wiley rode down the long string of wagons, looking for Hendricks. He found him near the end of the caravan, and he could swear the man's eyes turned red with suspicion. He passed three of Dorsett's wagons before he found Hendricks, and the tail flaps on a couple of them weren't tightly secured, letting him glance into the beds. He could swear the wagons were almost empty. It didn't make sense, dragging them all this distance for the few goods they carried. Maybe it had been a sorry trip for Dorsett and Hendricks, and he wondered if they were still together. But

Hendricks was headed for Chihuahua City. Did he plan on another meeting with Dorsett?

Wiley turned his horse and rode beside the wagon Hendricks was in. Hendricks gave him no acknowledgment of his greeting.

"What the hell do you want?" he growled.

"I don't want any trouble," Wiley said earnestly. "I just want to get a message to Dorsett—and Linda." He was surprised at how easily the name came out. A while back, it would have stuck in his throat.

He could be mistaken, but he thought some flicker of fright shone in Hendricks' eyes. He wasn't wrong about the sweeping wash of color in his face.

"I told you before I didn't know where Dorsett was. I don't expect to see him again. I'm just taking care of my business, trying to get my wagons through."

Wiley looked steadily at him. You're a liar, he thought; something touched you on the quick, and it showed. He was hiding something, and Wiley didn't give a damn what it was. But he could abandon hope of Hendricks giving Dorsett any kind of a message.

He lifted the reins, and Hendricks stabbed a finger at him. "You come nosing around my wagons again, and I promise you it'll get you a bullet in the head."

A dozen rejoinders flashed through Wiley's

head, but he didn't say any of them. All of his contacts with Hendricks had been sorry; he didn't intend there should be any more of them.

Hendricks' bullwhackers must have sensed the abrasion between them, for they jeered Wiley as he passed the wagons. He ignored them.

Elam looked curiously at him when he rejoined the column, but he didn't comment.

Valverde was in the bottoms, and Doniphan made a semipermanent camp and spent some time there. It wasn't just this march that had worn out the troops; it was the cumulative effect of all the steps they had taken. They looked like hell, their uniforms were in rags, and most of them wore long beards. Too many of them had typhoid or scurvy, and they were yellow faced and shivering. The pale winter sun didn't have enough force to warm men who desperately wanted it.

Doniphan never lost his grip on them. This was the point where the volunteers could fly into a million pieces, but Doniphan's patience never wavered. He had steel beneath it, and somehow the knowledge of it bolstered a man.

The rest was badly needed. Doniphan didn't allow them to let down too far. He insisted that the regiment look like soldiers. The tent shelters were kept in a straight line, and the debris picked up. That didn't take too much of a man's time; the rest of it was his own.

Elam watched Wiley shred the willow bark he had gathered. He had tried it, and it made a poor smoke. He gazed up the company street at Doniphan's tent. Officers were constantly going in and out of it.

"Another rumor's going around, Wiley. Doniphan got a dispatch from General Wood that there's a big Mexican force at El Paso. He orders that the march to Chihuahua City be abandoned."

Wiley rolled a sorry-looking cigarette. Now, if he could only get this damned bark to burn. He lit it, and it spit sparks all over his front. In beating them out he forgot about the cigarette, and it spilled its tobacco. He threw the paper from him in disgust.

"What do you think Doniphan will do?"

The tent shelter was cutting off the weak sun, and Elam moved to be full in it again. "He started out for Chihuahua City. I'm saying he'll keep on."

Wiley nodded agreement. That Doniphan was a determined man. He wished he had some chewing tobacco. He didn't know anybody who had any left.

"Who was that outfit that came in today, Daniel?"

"They picked out a fancy name for themselves. The Chihuahua Rangers, a hundred and three men who just arrived from Santa Fe. I guess Doniphan was waiting for them. I hear we're leaving tomorrow."

"We're getting deeper into the Mexes' country, Daniel. They've got to pick a place, if they intend trying to stop us."

There was a sober look on Elam's face. "I'm saying they've picked it out. We'll find out soon enough."

A man couldn't help but think about it. But if he thought about it too long, it left him depressed.

Doniphan left Valverde on the nineteenth of December. Ninety miles of desert was ahead of them. The Mexicans called it Dead Man's march, and after a half-day of stumbling through it, Wiley saw why. There was only one water place in it and no wood. He saw nothing that could be called graze. The supply wagons would be drawn on heavily tonight for hay and grain.

Men grumbled at Doniphan's relentless pace, but the verbal protest was the only one. They pushed hard to get through, or they wouldn't get through at all. Wiley cursed this country. It was nothing but misery to a man one way or another.

He could only believe they were through it when he saw the sluggish yellow stream. Man and animal could have all they wanted. He changed that to needed.

Elam nudged him. "Something big up."

Doniphan was talking to a mounted Mexican. Wiley had never seen a bigger sombrero, and his cart-wheel spurs were twice as big as silver dollars. He gesticulated eloquently, and a rapid stream of words poured out of his mouth. Doniphan must have understood some of it, for he kept nodding.

"I wonder what that's about," Elam said.

Wiley shrugged. If it concerned them, they would hear it soon enough. "Right now, I've got something to eat more on my mind."

That evening Doniphan ordered an issue of fifteen cartridges to every man. Wiley stared at them before he put them in his pocket. They had been issued cartridges before, but it hadn't meant anything. But that had been under Kearny, and Doniphan wasn't Kearny.

"I guess this means we're up against something."

Elam had a pinched look about his mouth. "Do you know what date this is, Wiley?"

Wiley shook his head. He didn't have the slightest idea.

"The twenty-fourth of December. The day before Christmas."

Wiley started to wish him a Merry Christmas, but on second thought held it. He was afraid Elam would think he was trying to put a sorry humor in the wish. He couldn't see any kind of humor in it at all.

SEVENTEEN

A report said the Mexicans were marching toward them, but Doniphan wasn't waiting for them. On Christmas Day they marched twelve miles. Wiley cursed this country as he rode through it. It seemed as though that was all he was doing any more. If it wasn't desert country, it was brushy country, and all of it had thorns that plucked at man's hide. Elam grinned, and Wiley transferred his raving to him.

"Goddam it, Daniel. Hasn't my uniform got enough rips in it already?"

Elam glanced at his uniform, then at Wiley's. Wiley's face burned as he got the comparison. He wasn't in nearly as bad shape as Elam was.

Donaphan halted the march and ordered an early camp made near a sandy island that made a fork in the river. The smaller branch of the river that went around to the east of the island was called Brazito, or Little Arm. Thorny chaparral thickets covered the marshland and hummocks of sand between road and river. Doniphan must have thought this place was a good one to make a stand, for the sergeants started bawling out the orders. Wood details were put to hunting for sticks in the brush, and sticks were about all they found. Wiley considered himself lucky not to be put on one of them. Nothing drove him wilder than to hunt honestly and hard and not come up with more than a few sticks.

He got put on the advance party just behind the scouts. An odd tingling was in his skin. He couldn't see a thing, but he had the feeling of action near.

Elam and Shannon rode on either side of him, and he pondered over the change in his feelings. He had felt close to Elam from the start, but he hadn't felt that way about Shannon. He caught Shannon's eyes on him and grinned at him. Army association sure altered a man's snap judgment about another. His original evaluation still held, Shannon was a brawler and a roughneck, but it was good to have him with instead of against you.

"Hey, look at that," Shannon yelled.

Wiley felt like gulping as he saw the dust cloud Shannon pointed out. It was lifting sluggishly and forming over the flatland to the south, and more of it boiled up and moved forward as a man watched. In just that short interval it grew bigger and bigger. A man still couldn't see what made it, but he didn't have to.

Wiley tried to spit to lubricate his tight throat. It didn't do much good. He tried to speak off-handedly and couldn't quite get the squeak out of it. "I'd say that dust cloud is about army size. And it sure as hell ain't made by any of us."

Elam's grin was too thin. "Then we'd better be getting back."

They started out in an orderly withdrawal; it was a pounding return before they went very far. General assembly was blowing when they reached the regiment at the river. A man felt good to see all that activity. Everything was frenzied movement, but Wiley thought it moved in slow motion. The corporals were distributing the company flags, and Wiley saw a man trying to load a Yager muzzle loader. He kept spilling powder and lost three patches, and Wiley laughed. Companies were forming on their own guidons, and the traders were forting up the Conestogas, yelling at and lashing the oxen. The dust they raised was a thick curtain. They were going to have to protect their own wagons, and Wiley wondered if the coming contact was tightening up their guts.

The dust cloud from the south kept coming, and it was big enough to darken the sky. Wiley first picked out the ranks of the Mexicans as a kaleidoscopic surge of colors, then he could pick out the individuals as they drew closer. The Mexicans, in the front ranks, had blue pants and red coats, and they looked sharp compared with the First Missourians. The Vera Cruz dragoons were on the Missouri left, and Wiley could see the dancing of the horses and the glint on their hides. The dragoons wore tall, brass-plated caps with buffalo-tail plumes, and the lance tips were down in a long line. Light reflected in little flashes from those tips.

The long line of Mexicans seemed to stretch from horizon to horizon. By God, there were a lot of them. Wiley glanced down for a pebble to put into his mouth, anything to suck on and maybe pull a little moisture from it. He didn't look too much; he didn't dare take his eyes off the Mexicans.

All of the Missourians were afoot, and the horses were led into the traders' forted wagons. Buckley bawled out the orders to count off, and Wiley was a number one. The number ones would stand, the twos kneel. Every man would hold his fire until the order came.

The Mexicans stopped three hundred yards away. At that distance they shouldn't look this big. Wiley said, "What the hell!" as a single rider broke from the Mexican ranks and galloped toward the Missourians. He carried a black flag on a long staff booted in his stirrup.

"What's he doing?" Wiley asked.

Elam gave him that brief baring of his teeth that carried no mirth. "You can bet it's no invitation."

Wiley's wrath stirred at the cockiness of the Mexican officer. He rode up to where Doniphan stood and skidded his horse to a stop that fanned sand out over Doniphan. He needs some mannering, Wiley thought.

The conference didn't last very long. Wiley thought there was anger on the Mexican's face. There certainly was in the manner he whirled the horse around and whipped the flag back and forth as he rode off.

Word came down from man to man, and its relaying was followed by hooting laughter. That Mexican General Ponce de Leon had sent over orders for Doniphan to appear before him. Doniphan's refusal was so doctored that it carried only the most vulgar language. Men laughed and laughed. Nothing better could have happened to break the tension.

The Mexicans started forward again. Skirmishers moved out from the line, and Wiley saw dark forms dart ahead in furious dashes, then disappear in the chaparral or hiding behind hummocks. Black powder smoke was beginning to puff up all over. A man standing three places down from Wiley uttered a hoarse cry and pitched forward.

Buckley's sharp order stopped the volunteers from breaking ranks to help the wounded man. "Hold where you are," he yelled. "The medics will get to him."

Wiley had seen the red patch blossom on the man's shirt. His quick-rising anger didn't leave any room for the nervousness.

The Mexicans were close enough now for him to pick out small details. Goddam! Who would believe that? That Mex infantry was barefoot. Their feet must be tough to be running across this ground.

The Mexicans had a single howitzer, and it coughed out an occasional hoarse grunt. Wiley could hear the passage of the shells overhead, but they were landing harmlessly behind them.

The dragoons picked up speed, going from a walk to a trot, to a full gallop. They made a solid front of red coats, and their brass-plated helmets jerked back and forth. A man kept his eyes riveted on those metal-pointed lances.

The Missourians fired in volley, the standing rank first, then the kneeling rank. If anybody was rattled by the charge, it didn't show in their shooting. The fire was deadly, cutting great swaths in the Mexican cavalry. Mounted men disappeared amidst plunging horses and threshing hoofs. Human and equine screaming had an odd blending note until a man wasn't sure which was which. Wiley saw half of a man's face disappear as he threw his lance up into the air. He sat his saddle for a couple of jumps, then sagged off to one side.

Wiley loaded and fired by commands. For a moment, he thought the dragoons were going to get all the way to the volunteer line ahead of them. Then the charge broke up against the deadly attrition of the Missouri fire. The dragoons wheeled in panic and galloped away. Riderless horses pounded alongside the mounted ones. Wiley picked out the little mounds of downed horses and men. Some of the horses tried to rise, and a few men tried to drag themselves away, but most of the figures were motionless.

The dragoons' breaking left the infantry flank wide open. Doniphan had kept a mounted reserve, and it galloped out from behind the lines and swung over to hit the infantry. The cavalry struck the Mexican line and cut holes in it with their sabers. Wiley saw a man split from scalp to chin and fall lifeless. The Mexicans floundered in the marshy ground not twenty feet from where Doniphan had chosen to make his stand. Mexican officers yelled and screamed, even hitting out with their own sabers, trying to bring some semblance of order out of the chaos. The Mexican infantry didn't have enough discipline even to hear the orders. Wiley felt a vague pity for them. If a man couldn't afford shoes, he was a peon, and to the peons the fear of the Americans was greater than fear of their officers.

The pressure on them never eased, and the infantry shattered under it. In another moment it was in wild flight, throwing away the impeding weight of the rifles. The traders were adding a withering fire from the wagons, and the fleeing infantry melted under it.

The volunteers broke forward in a concentrated surge, and the bugles recalled them. Additional pursuit of the Mexicans would only increase the slaughter. All around Wiley men danced, their mouths wide with their yelling, though he couldn't make sense out of most of the noise. He threw his arms around Elam, yanking him one way, then another, and he was as crazy with jubilation as all the men around him.

Elam finally got him to stop, and he panted for air. He caught his breath, and his face sobered. He looked out over the battlefield. "Wiley, that cost them dear."

Elam's mood caught up with Wiley, and its weight was oppressive. "A man gets filled up on the fighting, Daniel, and he doesn't think about anything else."

He was as drained as though he had been running a solid hour, and it hadn't cost that much physical exertion. It didn't take much to load a rifle and pull its trigger. He decided it had to be the emotion pouring out of a man that wore him out.

He saw the occasional blue uniform that was down. "Some of ours got hit, Daniel."

It took a long time to police the field. The American causalities weren't as bad as feared. Eight of the volunteers had been wounded. Not one of them had been killed, and it was a miracle to marvel at. The wounded were gathered in company wagons. The Mexican loss was staggering. Seventy of them had been killed and more than twice that number had been wounded. It put a tremendous burden on the surgeon and his assistants. They weren't equipped either physically or with supplies to take care of such appalling numbers.

A lot of the volunteers were called upon to offer what help they could give. As Wiley's weariness increased, it blanked out the horror. Some of the wounded waited too long for help, and Wiley could watch them die with fatigue-dulled eyes and not feel too much.

Elam was staggering under the same load. Wiley remembered him fretting over the question, could he kill a man. Elam could answer it now, and Wiley was sure the answer didn't haunt him.

EIGHTEEN

Doniphan broke camp the next morning, and the volunteers marched with loaded weapons and scouts out ahead of them. Wiley wondered if Doniphan expected more fight out of the Mexicans after yesterday's licking, but he knew that the colonel was a prudent man, leaving nothing to chance.

They marched to a location six miles north of El Paso. If the Mexicans were expected to make a stand, somewhere around here would be the spot, for they would be defending a large town. The river flowed between the shoulders of two barren mountains, and Wiley surveyed it with a quizzical eye. He was no tactician, but he would say this country would be tough to take away, if another man was as equally determined to hold it.

A Mexican party met them here, but there was no doubt as to their intent. Several of them carried white flags, and there was abject begging in faces and gestures.

Doniphan and his staff conferred with them while the rest of the volunteers waited. Good news filtered down to them. The Battle of Brazito had broken the last remnant of Mexican morale, and Doniphan was negotiating a truce with them. Doniphan must have been convinced that the Vera Cruz dragoons had pulled clear back to Chihuahua City and the militia infantry disbanded, for the scouts were pulled back and the rifles unloaded.

They crossed the river and marched into El Paso. Elam had the information, from some source, that four thousand people were in the broad valley. This was the most prosperous country Wiley had looked at since he left Kansas. Irrigation ditches watered cornfields, orchards, and vineyards. Mexicans stood in doorways, or lounged against adobe-brick walls. Many of them displayed bloody bandages, and Wiley knew they must have come from Brazito. These people would not meet his eyes, but he saw hating in their faces before they looked away.

Doniphan set up their camp on the flats south of the plaza, and Wiley hoped that the marching was over, at least for a few days.

The traders took every advantage to grab at the chance of business. The Conestogas were parked three-deep about the plaza, and the townspeople were hungry to trade. They snatched up everything the traders offered; bolts of calico, tin-framed mirrors, and bowie knives were prized items. People stood in long lines to work their way up to the wagons. The hating remained in their faces, but they traded.

Wiley watched the activity before he filled his bull-hide bucket. He was glad he didn't have to trade with those hate-filled eyes.

Something odd struck him. Hendricks and his five wagons were back at the camp. Why had he made no attempt to park near the plaza to join in the trading? If he wasn't interested in the trading, why had he come all this way? Wiley scowled. Hendricks would have been better off to have remained in Santa Fe. He remembered looking into several of the wagons, and they had looked empty, or nearly so. Hendricks could make no profit rolling empty wagons all over the country. What was Hendricks up to? The question kept sticking Wiley like a nasty burr. If Buckley didn't keep him too busy, he might keep part of his eye on Hendricks.

A fire felt good in the chilly night's wind. Buckley had kept Wiley occupied, and he hadn't had the opportunity to pick up talk like the others had. A lot of them were complaining about eye trouble caused by the scouring, wind-blown sand. Ben Marshall claimed the surgeon had given him sulphate for it, and it had cleared up his eyes.

Shannon had a pipe line to Buckley, and Buckley got most of the news that came out of Doniphan's tent. The colonel was going to stay here, at least until Major Clark brought up his battery. They were supposed to be three days behind, and Doniphan wanted those hundred and seventeen men and guns.

Shannon bit into a fresh chaw. "Doniphan's

kinda fretting he's got no news of Colonel Price. He wants that battalion."

Wiley put a fresh stick on the fire. "That sounds like Aleck expects another big battle."

"We'll hand them some more of the same," Shannon said comfortably.

Wiley had observed a level of the Mexicans' courage. If it hadn't risen any higher, it wouldn't be much more of a battle. Just the same, he wished it was behind them instead of ahead.

He got up and left the others. He wanted to look at Hendricks' wagons again. Every time he thought of them, he felt that prickling in his skin. He wished he could deny something was going to happen, but he couldn't.

He crept close to the camp site and watched the silhouettes of Hendricks and his bullwhackers moving before the backdrop of their fire. If they had any intention of leaving, it didn't show in the way their belongings were strewn around their wagons. Wiley had had a fight with Hendricks and a few hostile words at other times. Was that enough to keep a rancor bubbling in him? Or had his feeling for Dorsett rubbed off on Hendricks, and he couldn't recognize it?

He faded into the darkness. He scoffed at himself, but he would keep watching Hendricks.

The third night he saw Hendricks' bullwhackers packing the wagons. He wished he could crawl close enough to hear what they were saying, but the country here was too open.

He lay there, tormenting himself with indecision. He wished he knew where they were going; that could tell him a lot. He made up his mind. If he could get his horse off the picket line, he would ride a way in Hendricks' direction. He grimaced. He had chased wild geese before without getting his hands on a thing.

He grunted as he saw that Shannon and Marshall had the sentry duty on the picket lines. He didn't know whether he could talk one of them into letting him get his horse, but he had to make a move in a hurry. By Hendricks' frenzied hurry, it wouldn't be long before he was gone.

He jumped as a hand touched his shoulder. "Damn it, Daniel," he complained. "Why are you sneaking up on me like that?"

Elam grinned. "And why are you watching the horses so intently? Haven't you seen them before?"

Wiley started to give him a short answer, then reconsidered it. Maybe he wanted the backing of Elam saying he was doing the right thing.

He told him what was picking at him, and Elam listened. He asked only one question. "Are you sure it isn't because you're sore at Dorsett, and it's rubbing off on his partner?"

Wiley honestly considered that. "No, it's something else. I've got this hunch I can't get rid of.

Those looked like empty wagons, but Hendricks wasn't about to let me get close enough to prove it one way or the other. I'd like to get one good look into them."

"And we can't ask Doniphan for permission. He wouldn't stand for what would seem nonsense to him."

"We?" Wiley's face showed his astonishment.

"I'm going with you. I want to keep you out of trouble and get you back safe to camp."

"Sure," Wiley said gruffly. He appreciated it more than he could say. He needed the support of somebody to lean on.

"Tell Shannon exactly what we want," Elam said. "He's a thickheaded Mick, but don't try to fool him. If he feels he's a part of this, he's more likely to help us."

Shannon more than agreed to helping them get their horses off the picket line. He insisted on going with them. Marshall could cover them until they were safely away, and maybe until they were back.

Wiley tried to argue him out of it. "Damn it, Obadiah, don't you see what can happen to you? Doniphan will have you up on charges."

That meaty red face split in a wide grin. "No more than what he'll do to you. I'm going with you."

Wiley sighed and gave up. Nobody could change that Irishman's mind.

Marshall's back was turned every time a flitting shadow moved in and slipped another horse from the line. The three shadows led the horses quite a way from the camp before they saddled. Wiley was surprised to find how much he was sweating, for the night was cold enough to put frost on the willows. As they walked the horses along the river bank, hoofs made the forming ice crackle in sharp, snapping sounds.

Hendricks' wagon site was empty. "They're gone." Wiley didn't know whether to be relieved or unhappy.

"That's what you expected, isn't it?" Elam grunted.

Wiley guessed it was. He swung down to examine the ground for tracks. It didn't take much of a trailer to pick out the ruts the wheels made. Wiley picked up a handful of sand and frowned. These ruts were deeper than ones he thought would have been made by empty wagons.

He mounted and pointed toward the south. "That way. I'd say by the depth of the tracks, those wagons are carrying a pretty good load. I wonder what's the best way to go at it?"

"That don't take much figuring," Elam drawled. "About the only thing left to us is to overtake them and go through the wagons."

Worrying cut the creases deeper in Wiley's forehead. "If we find nothing, and Hendricks complains, Doniphan is going to have our heads."

Elam's snort contained no sympathy. "He doesn't need any more than he already has tonight."

Wiley loaded his rifle and heard the click of leading coming from Elam and Shannon. He might as well look at this practically, as long as he had gone this far. Hendricks might put up an argument against their looking.

This was like trying to get across a patch of quicksand. With every step, a man got in a little deeper. Shannon and Elam were in this with him, but he was the man who had started it all.

He started to lift the reins. "It's time to move. We should overtake . . ."

A rough voice hailed them, and Wiley flinched at its authoritative note. How well he knew that voice!

His face looked miserable. "It's Buckley."

"I kind of guessed it," Elam said dryly.

They waited for Buckley. If he hadn't been mounted, it wouldn't have been hard to leave him standing. His face had a malicious satisfaction as he halted his horse and looked them over. "So you talked Elam and Shannon into it with you. Maybe Doniphan will order you shot for it this time."

Wiley felt sick. He felt he had been on the verge of discovering something, and Buckley had stopped it. "What did I talk them into doing?" he snarled.

"Desertion," Buckley snapped. "I kept you in sight until I was sure. Now you're going back."

"You're crazy as hell," Wiley yelped. He tried to explain everything, and Buckley wouldn't listen. His rifle was lying across his lap, pointing at Buckley.

"We can't let you take us back now." He was surprised at how calm he felt. He glanced at the other two. "If he does, nobody will listen to anything else but the desertion."

Shannon edged his horse closer to Buckley. His rifle was aimed, too. "What should we do with him? Shoot him?"

That scared even Wiley. Shannon's face looked mean. "No, but we can take him along until we overtake Hendricks' wagons. If we find something, the damned fool might get desertion out of his head."

They boxed Buckley in from the back and both sides. "Don't make a fool mistake," Wiley said softly. "You wouldn't get three jumps before you'd be blown out of the saddle."

Buckley was more angry than scared. "Doniphan will never stop looking for you. I can promise you that."

"Oh, go to hell," Wiley said wearily. He could tell Buckley a dozen times that they would turn back as soon as they overtook Hendricks. Nothing was going to change Buckley's set mind, not unless Hendricks had something that would shock everybody.

They hadn't ridden three miles when the watery moonlight picked up the short string of wagons up ahead.

"That's who we're stopping, Buckley," Wiley said. "And we don't know whether or not they'll put up a fight. You can pull out your rifle to protect yourself. Or you can just let them blow off your head. It's your decision."

Buckley's face grew more and more bewildered. For deserters, these men were acting strange. "I'll ride along with you until I see what happens," he growled.

"Sure," Wiley said. He ordered a wide circle made of the wagons, and put on greater speed. It wouldn't take too much of a circuit to overtake the oxen's slower pace. He wanted to be waiting beside the road when the wagons came along. With a complete surprise, he hoped to take the wagons without any kind of resistance. If you find only five empty wagons, he thought, you're going to pay somebody a hell of a price for it.

They waited in a clump of corkscrew tornillo just off the road, and a man had to be careful of how he moved in it, or its branches reached out and grabbed him.

The waiting seemed like an eternity, then Wiley heard the creaking of the oncoming wagons and lifted his hand in warning to the others.

It must have been a horrible shock to Hendricks and the bullwhackers to see the dark forms burst out of the tornillo. Wiley had counted on the surprise being so great that it would wipe out all resistance. He was wrong. Even Wiley's cocked rifle didn't stop Hendricks. Hendricks must have some terrible necessity driving him.

He stood up in the wagon's boot, clawing for a pistol, and Wiley yelled at him, "No! Don't do it, you damned fool."

If Hendricks heard the words, he didn't show it. He was lifting the pistol from its holster when Wiley pulled the trigger. Hendricks froze erect a long moment before he started bending at the waist. He made an awful effort to keep from dropping the pistol, but he couldn't make his fingers cling to it. His eyes seemed as big as black caves in a white face, then he half-twisted to one side and plunged to the ground.

Wiley heard two more rifle shots from along the line of wagons. Then there were more rifle shots, and it meant that the bullwhackers had put up a fight too. His stomach was a queasy, bubbling hollow as he thought of the total; Hendricks and a couple of his drivers at least.

Buckley's words showed he wasn't one who had fired. "My God," he said, and his voice had a tendency to break. "You've killed three of them."

Wiley's nerves were close to the breaking point. He knew the number of dead men who could be laid at his doorstep. "Keep them covered," he ordered Elam and Shannon. "Buckley, help me look in these wagons."

His hands shook as he unfastened the flaps. This was the worst sickness he had ever known in his life.

"Anderson, I feel sorry for you. My God, you won't be able to go far enough to hide."

"Shut up," Wiley roared. He had killed men over empty wagons, and he couldn't take any more words from Buckley about it.

It felt as though a sour vomit was filling his throat, and his ears roared. There wasn't any use looking into the empty wagon, but he didn't know where else to look.

Something picked at him as a thought hammered at his head for admittance. Why was the floor in this wagon so high? It seemed twice as high as other floors he had seen in wagons, and a freighter wouldn't want it built that way. A floor built this high would cut down his payload.

He felt along the floor's edge against the wagon's side, and thought it was loose. "Buckley, help me." He was coming back to life, and his voice quivered. "I think these floor boards come up."

Working together, they could tilt up a section. Long boxes were packed tightly beneath it. Wiley had seen rifle boxes before. They were packed closely together under all of this false flooring.

Buckley knew what they were, too, without needing them opened. “Jesus Christ.” His voice was high and squeaky. “Are the other wagons the same?”

Wiley could grin a little now. “I wouldn’t be a damned bit surprised.”

NINETEEN

Doniphan's face never lost its stunned look as Buckley related the evening's events. "Five hundred rifles, sir. That's what we found under the false flooring." He shook his head in wonder. "And all I wanted to do was to arrest Wiley for desertion."

Wiley, Elam, and Shannon tried to keep their faces grave, but the corners of their lips kept twitching.

Doniphan looked at Wiley. "Wiley, how did you know those rifles were in the wagons?"

"I didn't, Aleck. But Hendricks acted so funny. The last time I talked to him he looked scared to death. I got a look into a couple of those wagons, and they were nearly empty. Why should a man drive empty wagons around? I heard Dorsett had gone to Chihuahua City, and when Hendricks pulled out, I figured he might be going to join him. What drove him so hard that made him want to get empty wagons to Dorsett? I just had to look."

Doniphan blew out an explosive breath. "It was a good thing you did. I'd hate to think of that many modern rifles falling into Mexican hands. What those two were planning is treason." His eyes were brilliantly sharp. "Now the army wants Myrick Dorsett as bad as you do."

"Yes, sir." Now his personal aspect of this had to come out, and he regretted that. The same motivation no longer drove him, but Linda was still a part of this. "I don't think she had a hand in it, Aleck."

Doniphan looked at him with renewed interest, and there was a fresh alertness in Elam, Shannon, and Buckley. He was sorry he had to wash his dirty linen before all of them, but he saw no way of avoiding it.

"What makes you think that, Wiley?"

"Because it's not a woman's business, Aleck. I doubt she even knew what was going on."

He thought there was pity in Doniphan's eyes and imagined what was running through his head. No, he no longer loved Linda. That had slipped away so gradually he hadn't realized it until it was all gone. The army's entrance into this would make it a public affair. He hated to think of her being so openly humiliated. He would like to get her away from Dorsett and send her on her lonely way. Maybe once she knew what had been going on, she would see Dorsett in an entirely different light.

"You'd like to find them before the army does?"

"Yes, sir. I'd turn Dorsett over to the army."

Doniphan studied him. "I think you would. But we might have to fight our way into Chihuahua City."

Faces around him picked up a quickening. It was Buckley who said, "You've heard something that's changed everything?"

Doniphan sighed. "I just received a dispatch from Colonel Price. He won't send the rest of the battalion. New Mexico is blowing up in his face. The Mexicans have started a revolt, and the Indians have joined in. They've already massacred fifteen Americans. Price reports that it's spreading. With those conditions I don't blame him for leaving Santa Fe unprotected. We'll get Clark's battery, the men with him, and no more. Now, what do we do?"

"Is General Wood marching on Chihuahua City?"

Doniphan winced. "One rumor says he's been wiped out. I can't believe it. But whatever's happened, it looks as though he's abandoning his campaign. There's a possibility he couldn't get through the Coahuila Mountains. It looks as if it's left up to us, if it's going to be done at all."

"Then let's do it," Shannon shouted. "Ain't you tired of depending upon somebody else, Aleck?"

Elam gave him a bright-eyed grin. "He put that pretty good, Colonel."

"I'd say we have to get to Chihuahua City, Aleck," Wiley said gravely.

Buckley had more of a military mind than the others. "Do you figure we can, sir?"

"I can make a military battalion of the traders.

They weren't involved in Hendricks' and Dorsett's treachery, and it shames them. I can make Sam Owens the battalion's major. He's a good man."

Buckley's breathing came faster. "How many men would that give us?"

"I've stretched it as far as I can, Buckley. I make it just over nine hundred men."

"Don't you think that's enough?" Shannon roared at Buckley.

Buckley never took his eyes off Doniphan's face. "I think it will be."

Wiley looked from face to face. He saw no fear in any of them. A hell of a lot of talking would be done around the campfires tonight.

Major Clark's battery arrived the first of February, and the whole town turned out to see him arrive. The Mexican brass cannon, captured at Brazito, was on display as Doniphan paraded the newly joined outfit. The talk said the First Missourians would leave in the morning. Wiley itched to be on the way. Their departure would end the drills, the saber exercises, and the cavalry charges. He particularly hated that, for it put extra work on the horses. The men might cuss and stagger under it, but they bounced better than the animals.

Chihuahua City lay two hundred and thirty miles from El Paso, and it was a forbidding distance. Wiley knew how savage most of this Mexican country had already been. Just thinking of that many miles strung out ahead put a pale tightening in a man's face.

Too much of this Godforsaken country was waterless sand, and the wind never ceased blowing. It blew off of the purple mountains ahead and seemed to accelerate each forward mile. A man rode with his neckerchief over his nose and mouth to keep the seeking sand grains out, and they stung with enough force to make his cheeks bloody. Water wasn't the soul-chilling fear as long as they marched fairly near the river. Away from the river nothing grew but the cursed corkscrew tornillo.

Doniphan was getting ready to turn inland. Wiley could tell by his preparations. Ahead was a desert the Mexicans called a *jornada.* Reports said it would take two hard days of marching to cover its sixty miles. Doniphan ordered every available barrel filled with water. That was the concern of every man, for no matter how much water they took along it was never enough. They had over nine hundred men to drink daily, and the horses and mules would take four times as much. Some of the men discarded their sabers and filled the scabbards with water. Wiley understood what they were trying to do, but they got only a pitiful amount of water. They would miser it as long as they could, but before they drank it, evaporation and spillage would put inroads into the meager supply that would make a man gibber in rage.

Two men died that first day, and Wiley thought soberly as he looked at the emaciated bodies that even after all the hard miles behind them, the two men looked soft. He didn't know their backgrounds, but he would bet they came out of the cities. A man didn't necessarily need the hardening in his body to endure; it had to be in his soul.

It wasn't hard burying them in the loose, sliding sand. The thing that outraged Wiley the most was the two ragged blankets in which they were buried. Death ought to bring a man more than a piece of worn-out material.

Doniphan said a few words over the lonely graves. He was a good man at this, but Wiley was glad when it was over. A man kept trying to shut out his thoughts, but they kept crawling through his mind like snakes. A man couldn't help but compare himself with the two sandy holes.

A man would never get any closer to hell than in a *jornado.* The traders had to fight for every foot their wagons made. The sand melted beneath the wheels as though it had no tangible substance, and three and four teams had to be put on a wagon to drag it through. Two of the wagons sank in over their hubs and had to be abandoned.

They clawed through the *jornado*, and each agonizing minute further dulled Wiley's senses.

A man reached a point where it no longer mattered. He went through the motions needed for survival, but they were purely mechanical. Animals were crazed by thirst, and some of the men went out of their heads and had to be tied down in the company wagons. All around Wiley, men cursed Doniphan and threatened mutiny, and Wiley mounted it as loudly as anybody else. In a saner moment, Wiley didn't see how Doniphan stood up under this and felt a guilty shame at his part. He had only to look after himself, while Doniphan bore the responsibility for every man and animal on his bending shoulders.

They got through the *jornado* by marching till midnight on the second day. Dear God, Wiley thought. It's got to get better. When he looked at the ragged and worn-out uniforms he didn't see how it could. He fell into an exhausted sleep, hoping the supply wagons had gotten through.

He wanted to scream in frustration at the news the following day. The quartermaster sergeant had jettisoned eight thousand pounds of flour and several dozen barrels of salt and meat. Elam said, "He had to, to get the remaining supplies through." Wiley wanted to swear at him, too, but he was too drained. Doniphan still rode at the head of the column, demanding that discipline be maintained. No man broke ranks, and he allowed no stragglers. Damn him, Wiley thought wildly. How much more does he think we can stand?

Seeing scattered Mexicans and Indians was an infusion of new blood, for Doniphan was able to trade with them. He traded for anything that was usable; boots were replaced with Pueblo moccasins, and coats with Saltillo serapes and Navajo blankets. Wiley grinned sourly at the nondescript appearance of the First Missourian. Troopers wore flimsy cotton pants and buckskin britches. He was glad he was lucky enough to get the buckskin. He didn't think the cotton pants would last long.

He thought there wasn't a laugh left in him, but it bubbled up in his throat and burst out of his lips. Elam looked at him as though he thought he had gone suddenly crazy. "Tell me what's funny. I'd like to believe there might be something funny left."

"I was just thinking how Kearny used to yell himself purple in the face trying to make us look like soldiers. I'd like for him to get a look at us now."

It twitched Elam's lips first, then spread. He laughed harder than Wiley thought possible. The harder he laughed, the more it gripped Wiley. If anybody came along this way, they would report two more men had gone out of their heads.

On the twenty-seventh of February the First Missourians reached the crumbling and deserted fort at Sanz. The scouts occupied it first and brought back reports of evidence of recent occupation by dragoons. Sure, it was the dragoons. Horse droppings were all over the place, but something had changed the dragoons' minds about making a stand there.

Contact might be made at any minute, and the army moved with renewed caution. An hour later, several scouts brought back two Mexicans. One of the Mexicans spoke passable English. "*Si*, Señor, the dragoons were under General Conde. He has withdrawn to join General Heredia's infantry." How many men? The Mexican rolled his eyes. "Many soldiers. Maybe more than four thousand. And twenty pieces of artillery." Where is this army? He squatted on his heels to draw a map in the sand.

He talked as he drew. "General Heredia has fortified the heights above the Sacramento River. Fifteen miles south of Sanz. They will look down on you every step of the way. They cannot be driven from there."

Doniphan gave the Mexican a tight smile. "Why, I expect we'll have to argue about that."

He passed new marching orders to his officers, and they repeated it down the line. Each time the order reached a new man it increased in volume. A sergeant couldn't talk in less than a roar. Three companies would make up the advance guard: the Chihuahua Rangers, Captain Parson's company of Missouri Dragoons, and Captain Reid's

Missouri Horse Guards. Some two hundred men moved out ahead. Wiley felt a little regret that he wasn't in one of those companies. The regret didn't last long; he would get all the action he wanted.

Doniphan formed the four hundred traders' wagons into four parallel files with corridors between files. The artillery and its six guns were in the center corridor. The First Batallion moved in the right corridor, most of them dismounted horsemen. The rest of the infantry moved in the left corridor, including the two teamster companies. The wagons were a moving fort, and Wiley said a fervent wish that it give sufficient protection.

He heard very distinctly Doniphan's final order. "We march at sunup."

TWENTY

Doniphan didn't miss his estimated time of departure by far. The sun hadn't climbed high when the column was underway. Shortly after noon, scouts came racing back, reporting Mexicans not more than four miles up ahead.

The column kept a steady pace south on the road leading to the Sacramento ranch. It followed on open valley, bounded on either side by ranges of brown mountains. As the road approached the river, the mountains closed in until they pinched the valley down to a mile in width. Across the narrow neck, from east to west, ran two canyons, one called Arroyo Seco, the other Arroyo Sacramento. Between the arroyos a peninsula of land formed a rocky bench. At some points the bench was several hundred feet high. The road climbed out of the arroyo and ran across the center of the bench directly through fortifications. The Mexicans had taken this height.

Doniphan halted the column a mile and a half from the Mexican position. He sat motionless for a long time as he scanned the height through glasses. Wiley was close enough to hear Doniphan report what he saw:

"One battery of four guns, two nine-pounders, two sixes on the point of the hill to the right.

Three entrenchments of six-pounders on the brow in the center. Another battery on the crest of the hill between batteries. I've counted twenty-seven redoubts thrown up and the infantry in them looks protected. The cavalry is about a thousand yards before the redoubts, drawn up in ranks four-deep. The Mexican guns on the heights command all of the narrow valley. On the east side of the bench, to block the valley further, they've built a stone abatis across the mouth. That bristles with guns, too."

Wiley strained his eyes. He couldn't pick out the details without glasses. Doniphan's report kept drawing an icicle down his spine. Doniphan described a tough nut, a nut that Wiley couldn't see being cracked.

"Storming that abatis would be suicide," Doniphan said. "They've figured us to attack by storming down the road. No, we'll go in another way. We'll turn the right flank. The weakest batteries are on that side. And there's only a fraction of the redoubts there."

Wiley had only one wish; that Doniphan knew what he was doing. At Brazito, it had been a far different matter. There, the Americans had the ground they wanted and waited. Today, they were approaching squarely into the long, bared fangs.

The cavalry would hit about the time the foot soldiers crossed the arroyo. The infantry could be too easily wiped out if it was caught in the ditch.

Wiley couldn't get one fact out of his head: the Mexicans had the height. They literally looked down on the tops of the wagons, though the troops in the center corridors were masked by the long lines of wagons.

Elam spoke as though something had just occurred to him. "For twenty years the army's protected the traders on the Santa Fe trail. I guess it's about time for them to pay back a little."

Wiley gave him a strained grin. "I hope it's the kind of payment we need."

Doniphan swung right and crossed the gully. The wagons lurched down into the dry arroyo and waddled toward the steep bank on the other side. The deep sand on the bottom was holding. Half of the Missouri Horse Guards had already reached the high ground on the other side. The Mexican dragoons had begun their advance. Wiley had a confused impression of shakos and pompons, plumes and buckles, sabers and sashes and, most of all, the lowered lances. This was the critical moment for the infantry. Clark was just beginning to manhandle his guns into position. The Mexicans were less than a thousand yards away as the wagons started coming out of the gully and moving into formation. Long lines of wagons faced the dragoons at an oblique angle, masking the American columns except for the cavalry. Doniphan must have signaled, for Wiley heard the artillery bugler sound his call. Clark touched off one of his twelve-pound howitzers; Wiley could tell by the volume of sound. He didn't see the bomb's flight, but he saw its bright flash as it landed among the enemy cavalry. A half-dozen horses were blown off their hoofs, and their legs scissored away in insane, useless effort. Three other horses raced away riderless, and the bright coats of men picked out the dead or seriously wounded dragoons.

The American six-pounders went off below the height, and shells cut holes in the Mexican ranks. Wiley took back the many swear words he had hurled at artillerymen in the past. These men were damned good.

The dragoons couldn't stand against the devastating accuracy. The solid ranks broke, and as horses were wheeled in panic, they slammed into each other. The first trickle of flight broke into a maddened rout and raced up the hills. The rout became worse with each jump of the horses.

The Mexican center battery opened fire, and the shells roared overhead. One of them hit a wagon still in the arroyo, and Wiley thought he heard the splintering of wood. A mule screamed in mortal agony, but Wiley saw no driver. Evidently the driver had abandoned a stuck wagon.

He winced at the roaring of Mexican shells overhead. He could pick out the hissing passage of every shell in his vicinity.

Each passing minute increased his courage.

Mexican artillerymen weren't worth a damn. They couldn't even come close to the range. The balls flew overhead or fell short and rolled along on the ground. He saw the first one bouncing and skipping toward him, and he couldn't believe his eyes. He pulled the claybank to one side and turned his head, watching the ball skip on by. This was the damndest battle he had ever fought, and he had an insane desire to laugh.

He saw Elam evade another rolling ball, and Shannon was grazed by one. All over the slope the volunteers dodged the Mexican artillery. A sergeant in Company D wasn't as lucky in his dodging. He went down, and his screaming was shrill. Wiley was close enough to judge that, by the odd angle, one of his legs was broken and maybe both of them. A couple of men ran toward the fallen man. The sergeant had help on the way.

The artillery duel lasted the better part of an hour. The powder smoke was a thick black fog, and Wiley could catch only a glimpse of the Mexican cavalry when the wind blew rents into the fog. The Mexican cavalry was in deep ranks behind their artillery. He was close enough to see the black leather shakos, the blue coats, and their scarlet turnbacks, the yellow sashes and brass buttons. They made no attempt to deploy into open order, and Doniphan's artillery was cutting them to pieces. Wiley yelled uselessly at them. Their officers didn't have enough sense to disperse them. He didn't see how the Mexicans could possibly stand. The pounding of the guns was smashing at his ears, putting a savage ache in his head.

He thought Elam had the same look of restlessness he felt. When would Doniphan give the order that would cut them loose? He sighed as the bugles blew advance. It was a relief to plunge into the coming action. The Horse Guards moved out on the right flank, the Chihuahua Rangers in the center, and the Missouri Dragoons on the left. The entire regiment moved to the right of the Mexicans to turn their flank. The white-topped wagons rolled in the wake of the cavalry, masking the two infantry battalions from the enemy fire. It had little effect, but a man did stiffen and fall.

Hudson and Parsons didn't charge with Reid against the center battery. The Horse Guards reached a gully at the foot of the ridge, and the Mexicans poured fire from the redoubts above. Horses started going down, and their pain-wracked screams added to the infernal din. Captain Reid started uphill alone, and Major Owens, of the traders' battalion, followed him. Everything was in complete chaos, for the men couldn't be rallied. Reid kept repeating a yelled order that was blotted out by the sound.

He finally made himself understood. He wanted men to dismount and prepare to fight on foot. The horse holders rushed in, and every seventh man took the reins of six companions. They trotted as they led the excited horses to the rear. Reid began to get some control, for the squads were firing in unison. On the extreme flank two howitzers pulled into position, and began to have a crushing effect. The foot volunteers broke out of the gully and surged up the steep, rocky slope. Every now and then a man fell out of the advance, for the heavy fire still raked them from above.

Doniphan committed the rest of his forces, and Wiley lost sight of Elam as he charged up the slope. A man could see the soldier nearest him charge on, or fall, but he had no clear awareness of what was happening on the rest of the battlefield. He couldn't say how the First Missourians were doing; he knew only that those around him still climbed.

He found Reid seventy yards below the first redoubt, crouching in a little hollow to protect himself from the fire above.

"Take my horse, Captain." Offering it caused Wiley a wrench.

Reid gave him a staring look as though he didn't understand, but he swung into the saddle and was gone.

Wiley was a footman now, and he wondered what had become of Elam and the others. A couple of volunteers plunged into the hollow with him. He knew their names and not much more.

He thought their faces were excited, but they weren't scared. Hell, fear hadn't touched him as yet.

Riflemen fired in concentrated bursts, and the rain of howitzers demanded their toll. These were Missouri riflemen, and they didn't fire needlessly. Every time they aimed and pulled the trigger, they had a target. The Mexican infantryman was afraid of that deadly accuracy. He crouched in the trenches, exposing no part of himself as he leveled the rifles across the breastworks and fired them without seeing a man.

Wiley yelled as they moved out of the hollow. They were moving again, the charge was beginning to gain increasing momentum.

Reid was up ahead and so was Major Owens. Wiley saw a shell burst near Owens' horse and thought he caught a glimpse of Owens lurching out of the saddle. He lost sight of him after that.

Men had insane looks on their faces as they reached the first redoubt. Wiley saw Owens again. Owens was dressed in white and lying dead across the first parapet. It put a raging anger in him. Owens had helped lead this charge; he deserved something better than this.

He plunged over the breastworks, and the trench was choked with Mexican infantry. Barefooted men in white cotton tried to fire or reload. Some of them tried to bring bayonets into play, but the trench was too crowded. If they had any determination to stand, it lasted only for the space of a few breaths. Then they were scrambling up the rear to escape the crazed American attack.

The greatest danger in the trench didn't come from the Mexicans; it came from the volunteers riding up across the parapets and dropping down on a suddenly terrified mass of men. Wiley escaped one of them by pressing close against the trench wall; another brushed him hard enough to stagger him. A barefooted Mexican lurched at him with an upraised machete, and Wiley side-stepped and jabbed with the bayonet. He spitted him through the stomach, and the horrified widening of the man's eyes would stay with him for a long time.

The flooring of the trench was getting bright red patches that were turning slick, and the smell of death, the smell of gunpowder and blood grew heavy and nauseating. The fighting was passing on to the next redoubt. The artillerymen got a single howitzer up the hill and unlimbered it in a new location. At fifty yards from the redoubt it raked the Mexicans with grapeshot.

The volunteers' charge had taken the pressure off the Horse Guards as the First Infantry Battalion stormed the redoubts on the left.

Reid was still having a rough time. The Mexican cavalry was making a charge that was pushing them back. Parsons led his Missouri Dragoons in a solid wave over the breastworks.

Wiley crouched below them and, for an eternity, all he could see was the slashing scissoring of horse legs overhead. When the last horse passed over, he dared raise his head. Parsons was hitting the Mexican cavalry, and Hudson and his Rangers joined him. Sabers glistened as they rose and fell, and the bright gleam of metal was dulled as they rose again. The Mexican ranks broke as that brutal saber charge cut great holes. They whirled and fled in every direction, and the running infantry, flushed out of the first two redoubts, looked as though they might be able to run fast enough to catch up with the cavalry.

The second redoubt was carried on a bench line clear to the east. The Second Battalion moved up the slope toward the Mexican center, and the heaviest Mexican batteries turned on it.

Wiley sensed the faltering of the Second Battalion before he actually saw it happen. He had no way of knowing what Doniphan's orders would be, but he could guess at them. Jackson was ordered to forget the trenches to his right and form his line of riflemen on that rampart ahead. All possible fire was poured into the center of the line. If it could be dented, or broken, it would turn this ebbing, flowing battle. The battery on Sacramento Hill was the Mexican anchor. If it could be captured or put out of action, it would stop that murderous crossfire.

A handful of Mexican cavalry rallied around the heavy battery in the hope of saving part of it. Ropes were looped around one of the guns, and the cavalrymen tried frantically to secure the other ends of the ropes to their saddles. If they could secure their knots, they might be able to drag the gun away.

Volunteers jumped another redoubt, ignoring the Mexican infantry shooting up at them out of the trench.

Reid sabered a Mexican Dragoon and rode onto the high ground. He had a favored existence, for guns spat flames all around him, and he never faltered. He cut the ropes on the gun with his saber, and it tore out the last heart of the Mexican resistance. The first of them spun his horse and spurred away in wild flight. Cavalryman after cavalryman followed suit until not a mounted Mexican stood his ground.

Clark had moved a whole battery to the lip of a trench, and the lowered, point-blank muzzles raked trenches with grape and canister. Men disappeared before the fire. Wiley had seen ripened wheat stalks go down before a sharpened scythe in the same manner.

Fear simultaneously touched the Mexican infantry, for they threw away their rifles and deserted the fortifications.

The plateau was black with running figures. Wiley tried to chase them for a while, but he learned something for a certainty; he couldn't catch up with a scared Mexican.

He stopped and felt the trembling of exhausted muscles in his legs. He was glad now he had given Reid his horse. If he were still mounted, he would be out there chasing other Mexicans. He shivered as he saw the running figures crumple under the swooping of a saber. Nothing seemed to satisfy the volunteers' demand for blood, for they chased the Mexicans far down the river.

The heavy guns had stopped, and only an occasional rifle shot sounded. Then they, too, were still. After the din, the silence was equally painful. It was so still that Wiley could hear the wounded groaning out in the mesquite.

His slackening muscles would no longer hold him, and he sat down abruptly. He stared about with vacant eyes, not fully able to comprehend what he saw. God, he wanted a drink. That was all he could think about right now.

He fumbled for his canteen, and it was gone. He didn't remember losing or giving it to anybody. He wanted that water bad all right, but the river seemed too far to walk to it.

Doniphan came by and leaned out of the saddle toward him. "You hurt, Wiley?"

Wiley tried to grin. "No, sir. My legs wouldn't hold me any longer."

"I'm glad to hear that." Doniphan used gruffness to hide the concern in his voice.

"We won, didn't we, Aleck?"

Doniphan couldn't keep his face clear of emotion. "I'd say we did, Wiley. More than I could even pray for." He started to move on, then stopped to add another thought. "When you feel up to it, Wiley, help bring in the wounded. There's a Godawful bunch of them on the ground."

Wiley couldn't resist saying it. "Most of them are theirs, Aleck."

Doniphan nodded. "That eases it some."

Wiley stood as Doniphan rode away. He helped with the wounded and understood what Doniphan had been trying to say. A man forgot nationality when he saw another bleeding out his life. The First Missourians came out almost unscathed. Major Owens and a sergeant were the only losses; only seven others were wounded. The Mexicans suffered a frightful carnage. Over three hundred of them were killed and at least that many wounded. Forty were taken prisoner.

Wiley's dispassion about them didn't last long. Every time he looked at them they appeared to huddle tighter as though they were trying to hide behind each other. The poor devils, Wiley thought.

TWENTY-ONE

The First Missourians entered Chihuahua City with Clark's band playing Yankee Doodle, then swinging into Washington's March. It looked like anything but a victorious army. Their uniforms were tattered, the footwear almost gone. But nobody could miss the gleam in their eyes, the proud cant of their heads, or the springy step.

"Wiley, it's bigger than El Paso or Santa Fe," Elam said.

Wiley still hadn't had the claybank returned to him, and Elam had had his mount shot out from under him. He walked beside Wiley, a different man than Wiley had first known. Elam had been through the fire that tempers steel and melts the wax, and he wouldn't doubt himself again. Wiley felt the same way. He might not be able to put it into words, but he knew what he felt.

Like Santa Fe, this was a city of churches and the inevitable palace. But it had something that Santa Fe lacked; it had a bull ring. The Spaniards no longer remained in large numbers, but they had left their influence on this country.

Wiley saw the same beaten attitude in the populace, the same hating in sullen eyes, but he doubted that the ability to strike back remained in these people. He would be glad when this damned parade was over. He was sick of looking at all these faces that wished only misery for him.

He tried to get to Doniphan right after the parade was over, but before he could reach him, Doniphan was surrounded by town officials and beaten Mexican officers. Wiley watched them with a cynical eye. They all want something, he thought. Now a new kind of pressure would start for Doniphan.

Buckley passed by, and Wiley caught his arm. "Buckley, is there any way I can talk to Aleck?" The frown was beginning to form on Buckley's face, and he added, "It's about the rifles. Aleck said to talk to him about them."

Buckley's face cleared. He had had a part in that, and he would give its final outcome all the clearance he could.

"Stay behind me, Wiley. I'll get you through."

Buckley had no respect for Mexican officialdom. He used hands and elbows, getting them out of his path. If he stepped on a too slow-moving foot in his way, he didn't mind at all.

He saluted smartly. "Anderson, sir. He wants to see you."

Doniphan's face held annoyance. "Not now, Sergeant."

Buckley lowered his voice. "It's about the rifles, sir."

Doniphan's face had a resigned cast. "I might have realized he would swing you to his way of thinking. Over here, Wiley. Buckley, keep these people from me for a few minutes."

He stopped after a half-dozen steps. "Don't tell me you've stirred up trouble already."

Wiley grinned. "No, sir. I'm just starting. I'd like to have permission to look for Dorsett."

"Won't you need help?"

"I don't think so. He might not even be here anymore."

"What if he's fled the city?"

Wiley sighed. "I don't know. I guess I forget about it then."

Doniphan unholstered his pistol and handed it over. "I want him as badly as you do, Wiley. You can do better hunting in a city with a pistol than a rifle. Don't worry about how long it takes. You're on official duty until you report back to me one way or another. Watch yourself, Wiley."

"Yes, sir." A lot of warmth was in that phrase. Doniphan was making it as easy as he could for him.

Finding Dorsett was the Santa Fe problem all over again, only much more involved. This time there was no partner left who might furnish a faint lead to Dorsett. Hendricks was dead. The wagons were gone and the rifles confiscated. Had Dorsett heard anything about it? If so, there was nothing to hold him in Chihuahua City.

He covered the streets on a hit-or-miss basis,

and the frustration built. He walked until his legs ached and his stomach was empty. He stopped at one of the market stalls and ordered more of the native food. The Mexican woman watched him with malice shining in her eyes. She was familiar with how inexperienced stomachs reacted to the burning spices.

Wiley grinned at her. He guessed his stomach was galvanized. This was hot but not too much to destroy his enjoyment.

Need for sleep drove him back to the camp. His blankets were worn and filthy, but it was dirt he knew. He didn't know what he might find in a Mexican hotel room.

He was back in the city early in the morning. This hunt for Dorsett made him lucky in one respect. In a day or two, the First Missourians would be back at the monotonous camp duties. Wiley grimaced. The drilling was the worst of all. In that aspect, Doniphan was like all the other officers Wiley had known; he believed that too many idle hours were bad for a man. Wiley decided that if Doniphan had a weakness, that was it.

The street was already crowded with people. That was the Mexican way, the busy part of the day in the morning, then again in the late afternoon and on into the night. The period in between was dedicated to the siesta.

His eyes caught the fascinating movement

of a woman's hips a quarter of a block ahead. They had perfect rhythm, flowing with the fluid smoothness of water, first one way, then the other, and he was lost in the delight of watching her. It was the rare woman who was born with that miraculous coordination of muscle and bone. This woman wore a mantilla, falling to well below her waist. Some clamor of recognition pounded at him. Hadn't he seen that proud carriage, the beautiful lift of that head before? Maria! It popped into his mind, and he rejected it. It couldn't be; she couldn't be here.

Now he had to know, and he quickened his pace. He caught up with her and touched her on the shoulder. Her face was ludicrous with incredibility as she turned.

"Maria," he said hoarsely and wrapped his arms about her. If this outraged her sense of propriety, he couldn't help it. He just couldn't control the yearning that swept over him.

She must have felt something of the same, for there was yielding in her, and he felt a wetness of a cheek pressed against his.

She remembered first, for she pulled sharply away, her cheeks flaming.

His laughter was completely free. It was only the ingrained teachings that formed her, not her true feelings.

"Maria, what are you doing here?"

It was curious how the telltale red remained

in her face. "I hadn't heard from Perea for so long. The unknown and the waiting drove me crazy. There was so much trouble in Santa Fe. The revolt grew and drew closer to me. The long journey didn't seem as bad as the waiting. Rufino drove me. I think it was a relief for him to leave Santa Fe too."

"Was that your only reason, Maria?" he asked.

Her eyes rose to his and remained fixed in a moment of honesty. "No, Wiley. Each day my heart grew heavier. I thought of all the fighting ahead of you. How was I to know you came through it unhurt? It seemed enough reason."

Her eyes were filming over, and they told him more than the words. "Maria, I am still looking for Dorsett. And my wife." His voice didn't break. "Now I have a better reason to find them." That put a quiver of anxiety in her face. "I want to set her free." He shook his head in wonder at how a man's road could change when he hadn't the slightest warning of it. "Dorsett is in serious trouble with the army. I hope he hasn't fled again. I only want to tell them what I feel."

He could say it honestly. He had examined his inner feelings, and he had hidden nothing, even from himself.

"Is Perea involved?" she asked in a small voice.

"I don't know. Why?"

"Because I think Señor Dorsett is the reason Perea came here. Back in Santa Fe I saw something in his head drive him wild, until he could no longer stay. When he saw me here, I thought he was going to strike me. He ordered me to go home several times, but I did not obey him. I stayed and watched him. Three different times I have seen him go to the hotel down the street. Each time, he stayed a long time."

That eagerness started bubbling again in Wiley. Had Yocupico been seeing Dorsett? "Did he come out with anybody?"

She shook her head. "Each time, he was alone."

"Did you ever see Dorsett around that hotel?"

Again she gave him a negative gesture.

"But you think it could have been Dorsett he was seeing in the hotel?"

She nodded, and that was good. Up to now he had had no more of a trail than a flying bird makes, but it was possible that the bird had landed and left a track.

"Show me the hotel, Maria."

She led him two blocks down the street. He stared at the hotel. It looked as big as La Fonda in Santa Fe. How was he going to learn who was in those rooms? If Dorsett was still here, was he using his right name? But if Linda was still with him, it would point him out. All Wiley had to do was to ask the desk clerk. It would work, if Dorsett hadn't paid the man to remain still. That was something to think about.

"Tell me where you are staying, Maria."

Her eyes seemed to grow more enormous. "You will be careful?" she breathed.

He nodded. "Yes." He didn't know what was ahead of him, but he tried to give her all the assurance he could. "As soon as I know about Dorsett one way or another, I'll come and tell you." He put a hand under her elbow and gently started her away. "Go, Maria. You don't want Perea seeing you standing out here."

She bit her lower lip. No, she didn't want that. She struggled to put so many things into a few simple words. "I will see you soon, Wiley?"

He smiled at her. "I've got every hunch of it."

Perea Yocupico walked down the street, and his anger was evident in the stiff-legged, hard-thrusting heel stride. His face was coldly immobile, but his eyes were flaming. He would see this Americano one more time. After that, nothing would remain between them. How the dog had lied to him! He wanted to spit the foul taste out of his mind. *Dios*, how the Americano had lied and tricked him.

He strode into the hotel and did not waste a glance on the man behind the desk. The first time he had been here the man had stopped and demanded to know his business. The fool did not make the mistake again.

He climbed the stairs to the second floor and rapped on a door at the far end of the hall. His impatience hardly gave anybody time enough to answer, and he knocked again, this time with more emphasis.

Dorsett opened it, and there was false heartiness in his tone. "Perea, I was hoping to see you today."

You liar, Yocupico wanted to scream at him. It was very hard to keep it bottled up. "I imagine you were," he murmured. Dorsett was doing a poor job of masking the anxiety in his face. The woman had it too, only it was much more naked. She sat on the edge of the bed and, after the first glance at him, did not look at him again. Something was driving her desperate. How bad she looked today! Daily, she seemed to be going downhill.

"Did you get the rest of the money, Perea?"

Yocupico's nostrils pinched together with the rush of his breathing.

Dorsett felt his cheek jerk. He had never seen Yocupico look so wild; no, it was more nearly a madness. "What's wrong with you, Perea?"

"I have just left General Heredia. He is forced to stay in hiding because the Americans have taken Chihuahua City."

Dorsett threw out his hands. "Can I be blamed for that? I fulfilled my part of the bargain." Maybe he would have been wiser to have left the city before the battle was joined. He had received only the smallest part of the payment. He had demanded that it all be in cash in advance, but it hadn't been obtainable. He had made the best terms he could, and he had stayed in Chihuahua City, thinking it impossible that Doniphan's small ragtag army could put Heredia to flight. But it had, and goddam it, nobody could blame him for that. He had gotten word to Hendricks at El Paso, and he knew that his partner had delivered the rifles.

What was Yocupico trying to do, cheat him out of his money? By God, he'd kill him, if that was true.

Yocupico had a sibilant hissing in his voice. "Señor, you made the big mistake by waiting. Did you think you would be paid the rest of the money without General Heredia waiting to receive the rifles?"

Dorsett felt as though a tight band was tightening around his neck. When he spoke, his voice sounded strained and husky. "What are you trying to say? That Hendricks didn't deliver the rifles?"

"They were not delivered, Señor. General Heredia received a report that Doniphan's army captured the wagons. He does not believe that."

Dorsett felt as though his eyeballs would pop out of his head. And he didn't believe any part of it. That Mex general was trying to blame his defeat on the lack of delivery of the rifles. It wasn't so, but Heredia could use it to save the remainder of the money and also his face.

The blood rushing into his face made the skin feel too tight. “You’re a liar,” he rasped. “You thought you found a handy hook to hang your beating on.”

Yocupico had difficulty with his breathing. “You a thief, call me a liar. Because the rifles were not delivered, my country suffered an ignominious defeat. And you are the one solely responsible for it.”

The man was mad, Dorsett decided. No reason could touch him now. He was glad he had strapped on his gun belt just a few minutes ago, before he went out. If he had any doubts, the intention was in the crouched figure before him.

“Don’t be a damned fool, Perea,” he warned.

He heard Linda’s muffled cry and didn’t dare glance at her. She could certainly see Yocupico’s menace, but it was something that only he could take care of.

Yocupico called him every foul Spanish word he could think of. Dorsett’s face burned. The ones that were strange to him didn’t matter; he knew more than enough of them.

His eyes were pieces of slate. “That’s enough.”

Yocupico had worked himself up to the breaking point. His lips were parted, baring his teeth, and that was a fleck of saliva at the mouth corners. Dorsett knew what Yocupico had been doing. He had never seen a Mexican who was too good with a handgun, and Yocupico had enraged himself past the point of accuracy. He saw the suggestion of movement in the hand before it actually dipped.

Yocupico was better than he expected. He had the gun out and lifting as Dorsett fired. The bullet hit him in the left chest, and it slammed him halfway around. Shock took the twisted hating from his face, and a reflex action pulled the trigger.

Dorsett heard the gasping cry swell behind him, then break sharply. There was too much pain in that outcry, and the instant fear tore Dorsett apart. He knew before he whirled what had happened. Yocupico's stray bullet had hit Linda.

She lay sprawled on her back, and a red stain was swelling on her bosom. It had happened very quickly, for her eyes were glazing.

Horror froze muscles and mind. He walked in the deepest blackness, and he was very cold. He thought he would never break through to the light, and this was what he would know for eternity.

He didn't know how long it was before he could break his chains. He spun around, and Yocupico was in a sitting position. The pistol had slid a few feet from him, and he tried to reach it. The exertion quickened the red flow from his lips.

No man could withstand that loss of blood, but nothing registered on Dorsett's crazed mind.

“Goddam you,” he whispered. He raised the gun and aimed. He pulled the trigger and saw Yocupico’s body jerk under the bullet’s impact.

Yocupico still sat, and his face was turned toward Dorsett. Dorsett was blind to the imploring in it. He pulled the trigger again. He emptied the gun with deliberation. He wished Yocupico was still alive and that there were more bullets in the gun.

Wiley felt the tingling in his skin as he saw Yocupico enter the hotel. It had always warned him true before. He waited until Yocupico went into the hotel before he moved.

He stepped into the lobby, and Yocupico was just at the head of the stairs. He saw him move down the corridor until he disappeared. In a moment, a room would swallow him.

He hurried over to the desk, and the clerk’s eyes were wide with apprehension. Wiley had seen his uniform put the same look into many eyes.

“Señor Yocupico,” he said. “The man who just went up the stairs. Who did he go to see? What room was it?”

“No comprendo.” The man shook his head.

Oh, damn it, Wiley raved. He *would* get one who didn’t know a word of English. He went over it again, speaking slowly and substituting every word of Spanish he knew. By the look on the man’s face he was only making it worse.

He stretched across the desk and grabbed for him. If he could get a hold, he might force him up the steps and make him point out the room he wanted.

The clerk evaded his hands and backed as far as he could. He gesticulated in a frenzy, and Spanish ran out of him in a torrent. Wiley was tempted to go around the desk after him, but he didn't know what the law was in this strange town. The clerk's voice was beginning to rise in pitch and volume. Wiley couldn't afford having policemen pouring into the lobby and arresting him.

He backed away from the desk, gesturing quietly with his hands. Maybe some part of that got over, for the man's mouth closed. But his eyes were wide as he watched Wiley all the way up the stairs.

Wiley looked at the twin rows of doors. If any noise had reached anybody, they hadn't opened their door to investigate.

He debated what he should do. Go down the hall, rapping in turn on each door and see who answered it? Or wait here at the end of the hall until Yocupico came back out? Which one he did would depend upon how long his patience lasted.

He stiffened as he heard the sound. It was muffled, but there was no mistaking it. That shot came from the other end of the hall.

He pounded down the corridor. He didn't know

from which room the shot had come, and his face turned first one way, then the other.

The next shot was a pointing finger. It came from his right, and before he fully turned that way, he heard another shot. They followed each other at spaced intervals. He didn't keep count of them, but by the time his hand closed on the knob, the gun must be empty.

He pulled Doniphan's pistol with his right hand, while the other twisted the knob. He gave the door a savage push, and his eyes picked up a confused and blurred impression. One man was on the floor, a woman was on the bed, and Dorsett stood, swinging a gun toward him.

"Dorsett," he yelled. Dorsett's gun was leveled on him, and Wiley had to swing onto target. His breathing lodged in his throat. He wasn't going to beat Dorsett.

He pressed the trigger, and Dorsett folded over at the waist. He seemed to hang there before he slid to the floor. Wiley didn't fire again. The expression on Dorsett's face told him how hard hit he was.

He kept the gun ready, though he could see no threat from Dorsett. He had lived through this moment many times mentally, but it had been nothing like this. He had been so sure he would know a brutal satisfaction at seeing Dorsett die. He didn't; he didn't know anything except that spreading hollowness.

Dorsett tried to smile, and it turned into a horrible grimace. "I guess I always knew you would catch up with me, Anderson." He could even find a wry humor in the moment. "What did you think when you saw me pointing a gun at you?"

Wiley scowled at him. Dorsett had a twisted outlook. "I did what I had to." His eyes flicked across the figure on the bed. My God, it was Linda. He guessed he knew it was, but it took a second glance to be sure. He didn't want to look at that death mask again. How different she looked from what he remembered! If he had passed her on the street, it might have been difficult to recognize her. Her bleeding, on the front of her dress, was massive. It had stamped her face, but something had been added to it. He thought a sickness had been building in her face for a long time.

He should feel some kind of grief, and he didn't. "Did you kill her?"

Dorsett briefly closed his eyes, and there was a new kind of pain in his face. "I loved her."

He said everything in that short statement, and Wiley could find nothing to doubt in it.

"Yocupico? Why did he do it?"

Dorsett had trouble focusing his eyes on Wiley. "We quarreled over the rifles. We were in it together before Santa Fe. He accused me of double-crossing him, of not delivering the guns. He was a patriot of Mexico." He shook his head, and it started him coughing. He sprayed a bloody mist before him.

"He drew and I shot him. It slewed him around, and his shot killed her. I emptied my gun into him. I only wish it held more bullets."

His eyes closed again, and a waxy, gray color crept through his face. Wiley thought he was gone, then the eyes opened again. Dorsett's eyes were dimmed, but his words, though faint, were still coherent.

"In a way I'm glad for her. I couldn't have stood much longer to see her grow weaker."

Wiley barely heard the last word, and he knew there would be no more. He straightened, and he was terribly weary. He looked about the room for a final time. He could do nothing for either of them except see that both had the nicest funeral Chihuahua City could furnish. Maria would want that for Yocupico too.

He did not want to think about Maria now, and he shut his mind to her as he went down the stairs. The lobby was beginning to fill with excited, yelling people, and he was too tired to cope with them. He knew how mercurial these people could be. He did not know what he would do if they got it into their heads that he was responsible for the killing in that room.

He sighed as he saw Elam and Marshall push into the lobby. "Daniel," he called. "You, Ben. Push your way over here."

He used as few words as possible, explaining what had happened in the room. "I've got to go tell Doniphan about it. Will you two see that none of these people get into that room."

Elam had a question in his eyes, and Wiley said simply, "The woman was Linda. My wife, Daniel."

He went by them, not waiting for anything they might feel they had to say. They couldn't ease a thing for him.

Doniphan had several of his officers in his tent when Wiley entered it. He put a sweeping look on Wiley's face and dismissed his officers.

Wiley thought with grim humor that it was probably the first and only time officers were dismissed in favor of a private.

"Go ahead, Wiley," Doniphan said quietly.

Wiley told him everything that had happened, not even leaving out Maria Yocupico. "Her brother was in it with Dorsett. Dorsett was in it for money. Yocupico was a patriot. He blamed Dorsett for the rifles being taken and tried to kill him. Dorsett killed him first, and Yocupico's wild shot killed Linda."

"Ah," Doniphan said softly. He waited a decent interval before he asked, "What are you going to do now, Wiley?"

"I'm worried about Maria, Aleck. Her brother

was the last of her close family, and she is a long way from home."

"I met her once, Wiley. Perea introduced her, though he resented doing it. A spirited girl. What would you like to do?"

"I'd like to see her safely back to Santa Fe." That damned color was beginning to heat up his face. He wouldn't be able to hide a thing from Doniphan.

Doniphan smiled. "Maybe that isn't all you hope to accomplish."

Wiley grinned sheepishly. "I didn't have much time to talk to her. But I told her about Missouri. If I had more time, I could teach her to love it."

Doniphan laughed. "If you can't talk her into it, you're not the Wiley Anderson I know. I could put you on detached duty to escort her back to Santa Fe. From then on, you're on your own."

Wiley's eyes were shining. "But the rest of the campaign, Aleck?"

Doniphan dismissed it with a wave of his hand. "We'll be marching east to meet General Taylor near Saltillo. I think all it means is another march. All of us will be out in June. That would give you a long time in Santa Fe. Haven't you done enough marching, Wiley?"

"Yes, sir." Wiley partially turned his head. He didn't want the colonel seeing his eyes grow suspiciously wet.

"Then what are you standing here for? Are you trying to make me change my mind?"

"No, sir." Wiley whirled and dashed out of the tent. No man would ever leave a tent that fast.

Center Point Large Print
600 Brooks Road / PO Box 1
Thorndike, ME 04986-0001 USA

(207) 568-3717

US & Canada:
1 800 929-9108
www.centerpointlargeprint.com